The King's Retribution

By

Ryan Keith Johnson

Copyright © 2007 by Ryan Keith Johnson

The King's Retribution
by Ryan Keith Johnson

Printed in the United States of America

ISBN 978-1-60034-558-6

All rights reserved solely by the author. The author guarantees all contents are original and do not infringe upon the legal rights of any other person or work. No part of this book may be reproduced in any form without the permission of the author. The views expressed in this book are not necessarily those of the publisher.

For information regarding permission write to
P.O. Box 195 Hammond, WI 54015

www.xulonpress.com

I would like to dedicate this story to Kristy.

It was dawn and the sun shined through the stain glass. The monarch sat in his throne with his head panned down. King Ruke Owen had a lot on his mind and was not happy with the past. Something tragic was buried in the past that provoked him, during the last years as father and ruler. He wished nothing more than the triumph of his country and daughter. He raised his head to watch the sun light strike through the stain glass of the sun and into his green eyes. The king could still hear his beautiful wife whisper into his ears seventeen years ago.

"Would you love me through sickness and health?" Queen Aarilinus whispered into the young king's ear. Ruke's hands slid across the queen's forehead and through her lovely, black, locks that streamed throughout the blanket. The hair was like the night filled with stars just as it was tonight. Ruke was more interested in looking at the queen than listening to her. "Do you know what I want more than power?" asked the queen as Ruke kissed her lips and looked into her dark, brown, eyes. "I'm serious my lord?" Queen Aarilnus' eyebrows raised. "What is it my lady?" asked King Owen. I've been holding a secret. I'm pregnant," Aarilina cracked a smile as she watched the king grin. "We're going to have an heir to the throne of Aria."

As the months progressed, King Owen spent more time with the queen and cared for her. They were inseparable and King Owen lowered his guard against his enemies. It was the day before the curse that set Ruke in motion, but until then they spent the time in conversation in their room. "A couple days ago you told me you weren't well. Why do you feel sick?" *asked King Owen as he watched Queen Aarilinus raise her shoulders. She seemed distant to speak about the matter, but prepared herself for what would perhaps dissatisfy. They sat upon the bed in moment of conversation as any other day.* "Do you remember the young man you banished from Aria?" *she asked slowly.* "The rogue warrior, what about him?" *answered Ruke as he sneered and looked away.* "He is in love with Olivia, our handmaiden and wants to make her his wife. Be merciful my lord, be kind, my king for it is only love. He came to me and cursed that I would die giving birth. He told me that because of your great evil that our child will die the same age as I. Aria will turn against a fool of kings and destroy the image of our royal family. Why are you keeping the handmaiden away from him? Why is he so angry with us?"

Owen's face turned to his queen as such eyes widen and eyebrows protruded while such young cheeks flushed red with anger. How dare this rogue come forth and lay a curse upon the queen of Aria who had nothing to do with the royal decision. He was King Ruke Owen and would allow those who deemed worthy to marry his beloved handmaidens. "Be merciful my husband for he has no quarrel with us only the promise to touch Olivia our handmaiden, for she has chosen him." "I am King Owen, I forbid any dishonorable man to set eyes upon my handmaidens or my wife. I have seen great things before I became king in my father's halls. If he really knew me he would not place a curse upon the queen which will cost his life," *declared King Owen.*
Queen Aarilina sat upon the royal bed speechless for she had never seen this much anger in King Owen. A piercing

in her side struck like the blow of a dagger from the thought of the rogue warrior. Never in Aarilinus' eyes had she seen such love burned away by the arrogance of King Ruke Owen. He raised himself out of bed like the creepy undead move from the dirt while such lips trembled in destruction. The queen watched the king leave the bedroom. She knew he was going to seek revenge with Adam Brokenheart. Suddenly the feeling in her abdomen became more than she could bare. "Jenna!" she yelled. "Yes, my lady?" answered Jenna, "It's time," answered Queen Aarilinus as she heard Jenna call some handmaidens to assist. The queen felt herself begin to fade away and hoped that King Owen would be merciful to The Brokenhearts.

A group of twenty knights rode on horseback to where Adam Brokenheart lived, which was deep in the forest. It was dark, foggy and the moon was full to light the way. Squirrels scampered across the trail as the sound of horses passed them in the night. Eyes watered and began running down his cheeks as the king felt the pain enter his heart. King Owen was the first to approach the well lit house.

Ruke jumped off his horse and pulled out the blade from its battle sheath. With the whipping sound of his sword, he slayed the sign that hung just before the door of the house. One of the knights looked down to see the sign read The Brokenhearts and turned to watch the king kick down the door. King Owen saw a family around a table serving themselves with hospitality. Five children looked up at the small army of knights who stepped behind the king. "You are the family of Adam Brokenheart?" "How dare you break down my door while we're eating!" exclaimed the husband. "Then you must be his family," sneered King Owen as he raised his sword, the mighty Ruke stepped forward and swung the sword through the table. The children and the mother ran for cover, crying and screaming. They were all, but the last Brokenhearts of Aria "We don't know where he is?" replied the man. "You call yourself a man you are nothing, but a monster!" screamed the wife.

King Owen turned to hit the woman in the face, with the broad end of the blade, and the husband as well. Ruke had never felt so much power driven in vengeance with a standing army of men by his side. The king would find an end to this revenge even if it meant destroying the house. The king raised his sword as though he was about to strike, but her husband would not have it and charged. One of the knights stepped in front of the king and buckled the man with the metal swing of his fist. The man fell to the floor and stared up at the knight as the sword was renounced from its sleeve, a child stood in front of his father crying in tears. "No, he's my daddy!" "Get out of my way!" ordered the king. "No!" cried the boy. "I've got a better idea." replied the king as he raised his hand for the knight to return his sword.

The knights fueled the torches and with the fire lighting the tips of their arrows the soldiers aimed their bows to the house. Twenty arrows flew through the air and set the roof on fire. King Owen watched the destruction done and still he felt his revenge incomplete. They heard screaming and banging from inside the door as smoke and orange fire filled the inside of the house. The challenger was not present to fall, but his family would be laid to rest until it would be revealed to the rogue.

He was Ruke, the man, the king, the conqueror, and the destroyer. Minutes turned like waves upon the shore and still King Owen hungered for power. The king shoved on with twenty of his knights and deep in his mind he heard the family screaming in cries.

The doors opened with the morning of dawn setting in and the king stepped through the halls, but they felt empty. His heart ached from what words his wife revealed of her passing. Was there more in this life before his time would come or would he be forgotten? Where was his queen to fill the halls with glory? Suddenly the young handmaiden with long, black, hair and brown eyes stared at him with emptiness. He felt his heart begin to sink and knew something was wrong.

"Jenna!" cracked the king, but all he got from his handmaiden was stillness like a pond with no emotion at all. There was no comfort to unleash from the young handmaiden's eyes. It was like she was carrying the weight of the world on her shoulders. "The queen has given you a daughter, my lord" her voice subtle and sad. "Aarilina!" cracked King Owen expecting everything was ok. "Where is she?" "She is not here," answered Jenna slowly. "What?" "She passed away in the night." began Jenna as she covered her mouth. "No" he murmured. "NO!" the king felt his knees begin to shake. "The queen died while giving birth to your child," she replied slowly as though walking on egg shells.

Suddenly Ruke fell to his knees as such lips began to tremble while the sound of metal echoed the empty halls. His hands sopped wet while covering his eyes that dared to grieve the queen's death. Except she would live on in the image of her daughter, his daughter. What was he to do now with his life, how would he carry on the hope of the beautiful nation? Knowing that the queen would be disappointed at what action he took to protect the image of the royal family. A handmaiden handed the baby to Jenna and took a couple steps towards the king. For seventeen years King Owen would watch over the princess until a prince would come into her life. The king raised himself from the wooden floor and gently held the baby in his arms. She was very beautiful, innocent, tiny and moved her little hand upon the king's thumb. What name would be fit for a child of his and hold such ties to the beautiful nation. "My lord, what would you like to name her?" asked Jenna as she noticed the king crack at the new precious thing to him. "She will be named *after Queen Aarilinus! Aarilina will never forget who her mother was. Aarilina will become the most desirable women in Ayana! My daughter w ill never be sick or weak and will inspire the men and women to live in peace."*

The green eyes blinked while the sun peered in from the window and woke him from such a terrible memory. Enchantments of the wind rustled against his ear and whispered words of Furrengee. The mask that enabled the rogue to achieve one of many beautiful handmaidens from King Owen. Sadness soaked into the king's eyes as guilt spread for what had happened seventeen years ago, but a king was to be strong and forthright.

The future would be shaken if the princess refused to marry the princes' that were selected. One man proved to match that worth by making it his effort to come for a full interlude with the princess. His name was Prince Tusk of Kalindor, he would arrive within three days. The king got up from his royal chair and made way to alert Princess Aarilinus in the Mid-Tower.

There was a brief silence as Animus soaked his mind with the face of the princess that laid next to him. They both sat on the bed and hugged each other in a golden hour like no other. It had been way too long since the exile; Aarilina could not stand another minute apart. She was wearing a lavender dress and had her hair down. She knew Animus was poor and didn't judge him on the plain clothes he wore as long as she got to see him. "Tell me this is not a dream," Aarilina whispered. "A dream it is! Which you shall never wake up," Animus's blue eyes sparkled as they soaked up her brown eyes and fair skin.

Princess Aarilinus bit her lower lips while the elevation of such beauty moved towards him like the setting of the sun. With eyes so courageous, his golden locks trailed to his shoulders and subdued the princess with a dreaming feeling to capture the moment in time. Aarilina knew him since she was a child in the woods and realized what to believe through the lips of Animus. "Do you promise?" The words embraced like the clash of swords. "I give you my word." The answer made way like a tidal wave.

A grin surfaced with the close of such stunning eyes, while Aarilina licked her lips in preparation to speak of activities that reached the mind of a girl. Suddenly the slam of a fist erupted through the door hinges and shot Aarilina with fright from the bed. They were invaded by the presence of the king. "Hide!" Aarilina whispered as she turned around to face the door. Animus looked around the bedroom with eyes wide awake realizing he was not in a dream at all, but inside the mid-tower. A dead end that meant hiding from the king would be like a man caught naked with his daughter. Suddenly a sneak gesture from Aarilina's cute, innocent, eyes directed him under the bed.

Animus slipped under the bed and felt the smooth, wooden, floor buckle against his back. It wasn't the comfort that challenged such fear for it was the coldness in Animus' veins that perspired the peasant with sweat. It had been six months since the last capture and he didn't want to be apprehended in the hands of the king again. "Aarilina is it too early to let your father in?" "What do you want?" she answered while turning the door knob, letting a crack surface from the door. She didn't accept the fact that father was on to her about Animus, but wasn't going to take any chances. Aarilina hoped that Animus wouldn't get caught.

King Owen entered the chamber slowly as Aarilina stepped aside from the shadow of the staircase outside her room while light from the window breached his eyes. The rich aroma of lilacs filled the room as well as the sound of robins chirping on the edge of the vine. "Father, there is nothing to discuss," protested Aarilina. Her eyes glared upon the king's eyes, then to his numerous gold necklaces filled with rubies, diamonds, and sapphires. With such endowment, she sensed the day where the stroke of his iron fist would tarnish the echelon of monarchs. That didn't seem to bother father since he was content on controlling her life. "I have granted the rights for the first man to proclaim fortune upon my house. Upon our last speech of carrying on the throne of Aria I have been making preparations for your survival." "Survival from what father?" Aarilina turned away from father to the bed and rolled her eyes. "As princess of Aria you are to wed an honorable prince and lead a life free of despair." "Really, father who are these suitors and what fortune do they seek that enables you to be rest assured that I will be free of despair?" she asked.

How could a princess trust the will of a father when the only intention remained was to use the power for himself. Aarilina felt father's body move towards hers as her navel faced the bed and window. The touch of a hand on her arm was slow as well as bitter. It was cold like death, but tickled her insides as memories unfolded in the appearance of a child. It was a day set in a passage of childhood dreams when a daughter's trust existed with the protection of peace, justice and love. Animus was here, thought the princess as she saw the vine tied near the window sill. He would not escape her mind so quickly, but neither would the thought of father. Princess Aarilinus turned around as her eyes wandered from the floor and looked into father's green eyes to see what truth lied within him. "Prince Tusk of Kalindor, Lord Corsair of Sporsindor, Lord Ruben of Endswood, Lord Domineer of Aryan and Lord Lordoriouse of Stalous are five of the men I've selected to go on this quest to retrieve the mask of Furrengee." "Are they young and handsome?" she spoke with raised eyebrows. "Very handsome indeed." "Are they tall and bold?" Aarilina continued with the grace of such lips. "Very tall." "Are they strong, loving and able to hold my heart captive?" "By what words would a prince be if he did not hold your heart with his," answered father. "What are they retrieving?" she asked while thinking of how to reject father's wide ideas to force her into marrying anyone. With an expression that was made to sin, she panned her face down to greet the floor while the ears pierced the air. "A mask worn by a great warrior that united our kingdoms as one against the dark forces of evil. I once possessed the mask, but someone stole it from me and returned it to the temple," said father. "I don't understand? What has this got to do with me? Father I can't be forced to choose the ideals of a man I don't know?" "Aarilina there is nothing to understand. You are the center stone to all that lies after me. The five men are powerful men who seek your hand in marriage." "Marriage?" Aarilina grimaced. "I choose virginity than your meaning of the word as I choose life of happiness than eternity of regret. Love is immortal as your meaning of marriage remains empty!" "How did you come to this conclusion when you've never been in love?"

replied father as his eyebrows raised and pupils dilated. "I have my ways of discovery," Aarilinus cracked with each syllable grasped by her lips. "I have found my true consort, through the days passed I looked up the word. The stories read, the poetry felt, the memories shared as well as the songs written and sung. I know of the word as it knows me." "If you're speaking of the peasant that I banished from our kingdom think no more than the dreams you conceive for it will poison you and the people you serve." "The people, or you?" protested Aarilina. "I'm trying to help you. I pity your irrational ways that will soon become no more. When the time comes of my passing the people will turn against you. Oh yes, my dear daughter there will be no comfort for you. Aria will fall and you will find your neck stretched on the edge of the guillotine for that loss of immorality with that peasant," said King Owen as his eyes stared into hers. "When I become queen I will bring love, joy, and happiness, which is something you don't do. The people will love me and will die to protect me as well as my consort-" "That is quite enough, daughter!"

Princess Aarilinus closed her eyes expecting to get slapped, but instead felt nothing. They reopened to find the cold stare of father pinching her nerves with his angry, red, face until the feelings in her body was gone. Father had never hit her in the past, but seconds ago it would have been known with the princess' faithful subjects. "Your in love with him, a peasant, a boy with no past and future. I suppose it was my mistake to allow the outsider to live instead of throwing him to the Dark Wolves?" "Father I have found my consort and you know very well that he is meant for me!" "Very, maybe you should explain why he is so true to you?" "Well, if you must know, I choose him because he is the one," her voice punctured the fabric of air. "He makes me happy when I'm sad, as his soul resonates with mine, I'm more woman than all the men I read about in stories and legends. When I kiss him I feel myself float upon the air as a feather flutters in the blowing wind of our world."

Aarilina's eyes closed and reopened to see the fires of hell stir in father's eyes. King Owen's cheeks blistered red as his right hand stuttered in outrage. She saw the king look away from hers and as they looked to the floor. Aarilina sensed in his voice the jealousy of a man once in love with her mother. "This man has no place in our country. The laws state that the princess can only marry a prince of noble title or from with right as the king sees fit to rule." "Surely not, I have read the laws of our country as well and as princess I can choose any man deemed worthy," answered Aarilina. "Not while I still hold the crown," answered King Owen while turning to make way with the thrust of the door.

The king was gone and left the princess wondering about a desolate future. With a kiss from Animus she watched him sail though the air and swing down the vine. Aarilina felt her heart escape the boundaries of the prison set before her as Animus disappeared from the bottom of the vine.

The day seemed to drag for eternity in what words could be seen to describe a world of sunsets as any other day. Animus helped Adam harvest the land for the last eighteen years, but hungered for adventure. The peasant put his blood, his sweat, and time into the crops secluded from the kingdom of Aria.

Memories embraced this young man's mind as the sweet kiss from her lips rekindled motivation to see Aarilina again. It would be days before the peasant would visit the princess. Harvesting the land became overwhelming and trading for food as well as money was becoming scarce. The family of nine barely had enough money to pay for the clothes on their back. They lived in a small log cabin, it didn't matter how they lived as long as they were together. Every night they would spend playing games performing on instruments using carved wood and stretched skin for tom toms, they performed as their own band.

The cottage was hidden deep in the forest just outside of Aria. The seclusion from the rest of the world rested upon Adam and Olivia Brokenheart's fear. One day the king would cascade through the door and arrest them and the seven children.

There was limited room in the cottage and the four older siblings lived in the barn, personally engineered by the architect of the family, Adam. His wife, Olivia, stitched all the children's clothes, blankets, quilts, and performed the cooking. She was a wise, but quiet woman that took care of the children. Animus struggled as leader against Sydney for he was the trouble maker and enjoyed arguing with his older brother. Gabriel, Aryan thought of nothing, but adventure as a part of life.

When things became slow and dry for Animus, Aryan and Gabriel looked up to their sinister brother Sydney who often sought more adventure than met the eye. The two sisters Jada and Alexandria stayed to mend the house and watch over their baby brother Erike. Jada felt compelled to seek the adventures of the trees and the animals rather than follow in her mother's footsteps. Now at the age of sixteen she strayed away from Olivia completely. Alexandria became the helpful guardian of Erike while their parent's were away for the day. She was the eyes and ears that warned her brothers and sister of incoming problems that were to be faced.

That evening Animus sat down next to Adam as always and ate with the family. Through many troubles and hardships the hospitality always worked out at the end of there hard work. Through the wits of Olivia's conversation with Adam of an unclear season. They spoke about Sydney's crime of stealing and animosity towards the king. "He's seventeen, there is very little order I can execute against Sydney without kicking him out of the house." "Then bring the law upon him," replied Olivia. "It's just that I'm afraid he'll drag the whole family into a big mess with the affairs of the king, which we don't need to compromise or teach Aryan and Gabriel to do negative things." "I'll have a talk with him," answered Adam as he scratched his nicely trimmed, black, beard. "Father what do you know about the stories?" asked Animus as he drove a fork into the carrots and potatoes. Adam turned his square head to the oldest son as he was about to take a bite out of supper. Memories of telling stories began to surface in the mind as Animus swallowed his potatoes. "You mean the legend of Furrengee?" Just then a break at the door interrupted the conversation. It was Aryan and Gabriel. They had returned from setting raccoon traps and were exhausted from their long walk. They closed the door behind them and took off their hats and coats. "Where's Sydney?" asked Olivia. "He decided to go into town to barter," replied Gabriel. "More like steal," answered Adam as he turned his attention to Animus. "You speak of the bed time stories of Furrengee?" "Yes! The stories you told me when I was young. Can you tell me more about the mask?" asked Animus.

All was quiet and Animus focused his eyes on the stories rather than the plate of food that was before him. His younger siblings began to laugh among themselves and distracted Animus from his thoughts. Erike and Alex whispered among themselves of their older brother's ambitions. "Animus is in love with the princess," boasted Alexandria with a big grin on her face. "You think you can mind your own business? If your not going to eat go change the stalls in the barn!" Animus' face began turning red with embarrassment. He should have expected to become a target for mockery.

Animus closed his eyes and had second thoughts about Furrengee even being a real person rather than a character in a book. Yet the mind wandered and wondered through all the stories that father told him, were they even true? All the answers in the world about a mask that held incredible power lay hidden in stories by Adam. "Son do you seek the mask for Princess Aarilinus?" asked Adam. "Look, just forget it!" Animus' lips trembled as he took a bite out of his peas and looked away. "It's silly you risk your heart for that girl, when the king strives to kill you," replied Adam as he crossed his arms and looked into Animus's eyes as level as a bridge across a river. "The king has sent a proposal to all suitors who seek my love in marriage for the return of the mask!" said Animus "You believe the king will honor his agreement?" asked Adam. There was a brief silence at the table. "Possibly," answered Animus as he felt a strange numbness in his toes that he made a mistake.

Animus' father set the fork next to the plate and rose up from the throne just as Animus stood up. The two men walked outside of the cottage and watched the stars glitter upon them. The night seemed remarkable from the ground as they saw it littered with diamonds. "Beautiful night." Adam let out a sigh, but suddenly heard a small nudge at the entrance and opened it to reveal the kids. Alexandria and Erike were near the bark of the door eves dropping to the private conversation. "Could you excuse us? Help your mother with the chorus," replied Adam as he pushed them away with his hands and looked at Animus. "I think its time we have a talk," answered Adam as he led Animus from the porch into the meadow.

Animus felt the cool breeze run through his blond hair and the night sky revealed millions of stars that sparkled, calling his name. It reminded Animus that every star had its dream and wish. Memories emerged of this strange surrounding. He could almost hear himself laughing in joy as he played with his brothers Sydney and Gabriel. The light chime of their voice arguing in forth rite to the imagination of sword fights. They both sat next to each other on a swing bench that was built in the middle of the yard. Father stretched his arms out as though he were reaching for the night sky and yawned. "Words are much more than action, they are not carved in stone. The king wants to use the mask for his own purpose."

Animus remained quiet as his eyes met with Adam's to search out the answers needed to find the truth. When there was nothing laid down in stone there would be no way to know if the king would be true to his words. Adam knew for certain that the king would have Animus captured and killed. "Then how will I succeed?"

Adam looked into Animus' eyes in ways of protection of a father from a course of destruction. The weight of wisdom and regret bombarded Adam with confusion to hide or run away. He only wished things were different for his son. It was a father's dream for every son to come out with a well drawn map of direction. Except it was Adam's worst fear for Animus' future to be with this insignificant woman that held his son's heart captive. This woman that was daughter of a blood enemy with a black and white past. "Forget about her! Forget your heart and runaway from her!" "I can't! She's the reason I live. Father I can't turn my back on her, I need to be with her, Aarilina is my muse."

His father remained silent and loomed his head towards the ground. Animus took a deep breath and turned away knowing deep in his soul he was facing a great destiny. Adam's eyes turned back up from the ground and met with the outline of his son's blowing, blonde, locks against the night. Adam saw himself and knew there was no way to talk him out of it. "Did the king give all you suitors a contour for the passage of the Furrengee Citadel?" "Yes." "The path will lead through many traps!" answered Adam.

Adam raised his eyebrows upon his face and ran his right hand through his beard. Animus picked up on Adam's expression and it was revealed there was hope. The farmer turned and stared at his own reflection many years ago. "Father, there has got to be a way!"

said Animus as he stared into his father's eyes. "There is a way," answered Adam with a smile as he dug into his pocket and pulled out a yellow piece of paper. With this yellow piece of paper would be the change Animus would be looking for. "This is a map of the fortress that will help you get the mask. There are more dangerous things in the fortress than King Owen. Are you prepared for that?" "I would die for her," answered Animus. The two men walked back to prepare for tomorrow's challenge.

A day without Animus was long and difficult for the lonesome princess. The monarch could feel the beautiful, blue, dress made of silk touch her ankles. Goose bumps covered her legs from the breeze of the cool summer morning. It seemed nice to walk the trails of the castle within endless acres of trees without worries from father. With permission, she was granted the small task to walk the castle grounds accompanied by her trusted bodyguard.

The clouds unveiled the hot ball of fire and its persuasion was answered to challenge such beautiful skin. Her eyes opened from the blindness to view the long, stone, path ahead. Hours seemed to harass the princess as she grew tired of the body guard living such a serious life as a constant shadow. It seemed that he was expecting a gang of ogres to bust through the trees. She felt nothing from him except the cold bitterness from the armor he wore. Why was he ignoring her? Questions asked would only dare to be answered by her faithful subject. It would rest on Aarilina's shoulders to break the ice and reveal that this princess would not remain silent. "Bodyguard we've walked around the castle gates for hours and you have not said anything of my new dress today. Is it pretty or does it surfeit you?" "Your beauty precedes you throughout the land. If your father should find out that I answer you he will have my eyes pulled from my head!" "My father threatens you for a harmless question of looking upon my breasts?" "Yes your highness." "Fear not my dear servant, look upon me as you would no other and answer my question," replied Princess Aarilinus with a warm grin upon the warmth in a future queen's voice.

The servant took off his helmet and looked up from the ground to Aarilina's face. He was a young soldier with green eyes and short black hair. Never before had he seen a woman compare even close to her beauty. The gorgeous, brown, eyes and long eyelashes opened his window to the true meaning of loveliness. Her light blue dress was silk with ribbons of gold matching the crown. The princess opened her moist lips and it looked like she was going to blow a kiss to him. When the chiming of syllables unleashed to his ears he thought he had died. "Aren't you going to tell me if you like what I'm wearing?" she revealed a fragile smile as each word plucked in his ears. He couldn't help, but look at her glowing skin that held such tender color to her face.

Suddenly the servant impaled himself to the ground as tears rose from his eyes because he had not seen such magnificence like Aarilina. The princess gently set her hand on the servant's head, touched his hair and pitied him. She raised her head up with a nod as the royal fingers brought his chin eye level with hers. "I dare to not look any further into your gracefulness for I will never face the king again." "It's ok our secret is safe. All I want you to do is answer my question, do you not like my dress today?" "I do not know, I only saw a glimpse and would need to see it again." "Very well," she sighed and rolled her eyes. The princess could not believe that father would punish him for looking at her. Something didn't feel right with the king, she would have to talk to him about this punishment. "You look lovely your highness." "Thank you. You see that wasn't so difficult." "No it wasn't," he answered with a turn to look at the ground and cracked a grin as they continued the long walk. "It's such a beautiful day! I like the way the clouds curl themselves into each other," she replied as she pointed to the sky. "It is," agreed the bodyguard as he continued to walk next to the princess and felt her gravity take over him. "No, your beautiful!" exclaimed the guard as he turned to look into her eyes. "Why thank you my dear splendor of light you sure have a way with words," Aarilina continued as she set her hand on his shoulder and proceeded on the rocky, stone, path that entered a wooded area.

Princess Aarilina had a wild idea to go swimming in the royal pool. The princess hadn't done it for months and it was a way to escape the invisible cage of the king. The slow illumination of her eyes realized that the body guard would have to be lost. The leaves rustled in twisted motions through currents of air as the aroma of flowers and trees filled her lungs. It was quite obvious that there were many hiding spots just in the trees alone. "Servant what is your name?" "The name is Sir Edward Bobbitt your highness." "Well, Edward I need you to play a game with me." Her eyebrows raised and a smile gestured. "A game?" "It's very simple. You lay facing the ground and count until you can count no further and then you try to find me." "I do not believe that is so, my lady, my job is to protect you. Not play games with you." "Yes, except my father wishes for my happiness. A princess can only take so much protection before she goes absolutely deranged." "I see," began Edward as he wiped the sweat from his forehead and ran his fingers through the thick, black, hair. They were alone and could easily sit back and relax. It seemed unwise to challenge the princess in order to have happiness. "What is the game you wish to play your highness?" "It's very simple my dear sir. Lay flat on your chest and count as high as you can until you can count no further." Her upper lip raised over her teeth as the brown eyes batted to wedge the trick over the bodyguard. "I can only count as high as my fingers so I'm afraid that I wouldn't be any fun." "That's no problem, count your fingers ten times and when you're finished renounce your fingers from your eyes and try to find me." "Ok," he replied puzzled with a sour sigh.

 The bodyguard laid flat on the grass and began counting his fingers out loud as he heard the light scuffles of footsteps grow distant. He remained unsure that this idea was the best plan to proceed with and feared the king was going to punish him. Princess Aarilinus found the pool and a smile emerged from her face. It was hidden in an old, unused, church that was transformed into, what she called, The Clandestine Garden.

 The water never changed, never grew cold, birds and animals made their way into the garden. They found comfort with the princess more than any of the other humans of the kingdom. The wolves, cats, deer, bears, fox, cardinals, robins and hummingbirds found refuge in the princess' secret place. "I thought I would never lose him," whispered the princess while stretching her arms and opening her hands to embrace the warmth of the gold globe. The head raised up to the chandelier roof and felt the life of boldness in light fill her gorgeous body. There were many visits before the trees, plants and flowers filled her sight with bloom. With the dip of a toe she felt the exuberance of light reflecting from each wave into her face. Aarilina kicked off the sandals, crown and untied her night color hair. The princess pranced through the shallow end of the pool and dared not to revert back as the innocent princess that the subjects had thought. She was tired of being perfect for father's self-centered image and wanted to be a dissenter.

She splashed the water with her hands, feet and slowly removed the blue, silky, masque and became one with the water. She rolled the dress up and set it upon the stone ledge so she could swim under water. With each thrust of hands and feet the lily pads joined the dance. They invited themselves into view when she came up for air. After hours of being relaxed she noticed the flowers were in bloom. Aarilina hymned a little tune and sprang up from the water to sit on the ledge. The long, black, hair stuck to her back as she felt the hot sun shine over such face and warm her naked body. Aarilina vocalized a song written for Animus as she closed her eyes and imagined him sitting with her.

> I circle around in the night sky
> waiting for you to arrive to me
> I got desire that burns in your heart
> it's what you want, it's what I need
> with the impressions that I must heed
> like magic it is
> like magic it is
> like magic it is
> I circle around the beautiful night sky
> I'm down to say this, sad good-bye
> if I can't have you I'd rather die
> but I know that your coming
> yes I do, deep in my heart
> from me to you
> because its almost like magic
> like magic it is
> like magic it is
> like magic it is

The King's Retribution

Princess Aarilinus' eyes opened as new flocks of butterflies flew upon her, unleashing the girl with kisses. One of the butterflies landed upon her hand while swinging its wings up and down. A few more landed and tickled the palm of such a beautiful hand. Aarilina cracked as she heard the slight beauty of the birds chirping for her to continue the beautiful hymn. The voice echoed like the sound of leaves and Aarilina's face reflected off the water like the fire of the sun. She looked around to see the roses and tulips begin a dance as the wind picked up. Two robins glided and landed on her shoulders, Aarilina cracked a grin while a shock rose up her shoulders with excitement. The princess lifted from the stone ledge and stepped halfway into the water. The chirping of birds pranced off her shoulder and next to a nearby stone. She splashed the water up in the air and filled such joy with the glory of dawn.

The rest of the day entailed of drying off and sneaking out of the garden to allow Sir Edward Bobbitt to find her. They would play a new game until dusk and join father with the royal feed.

It was drawing near to the time of the royal feed and all the knights were prepared to rejoice with Princess Aarilinus. Sir Bobbitt sat in his chair with twenty of the knights who thought nothing out of the ordinary. Edward Bobbitt tried to keep his mind clear, but couldn't. He was sure that the king was going to punish him for letting the princess out of his reach. At last the princess entered the dinning room with Jenna and took her seat next to father just as she always did. King Owen raised his wine to prepare a toast as he gave the bodyguard a dirty look. He slowly turned to his daughter revealing an evil sneer. "Long live Princess Aarilinus." The princess grinned as she spiked a broccoli from her plate and looked into the king's eyes. What was father up to and why was he giving her the sneer look Aarilina thought as she slid the vegetable through such fine lips. Every once in a while father did crazy toasts and flattered her with exaggerated dreams that were beyond her control. It seemed natural to expect a birthday cake in the mitts of things. "The future of Aria," answered the king as everyone cheered and took a sip from their goblet. Everyone commenced in conversations about the kingdom and how honorable the king was to his word. The princess looked around from both ends of the table and it felt like bliss

The King's Retribution

more than any part of life. "So what plans does the princess have for the rightful place as queen?" spoke Anson. "She is going to do the royal life long commitment that I've been waiting for since she was born." "Are we preparing to join any neighboring kingdoms for peace?" asked the middle aged knight, Sir Seres. "I wrote five letters to the kingdoms of Kalindor, Sporsindor, Endswood, Aryan and Stalous for a peace treaty." "Has the princess chosen who her mate will be?" asked Sir Norcom. "We decided that the challenge will be the retrieval of the Furrengee mask in the deadly citadel. The first man to return the mask will win my daughter's hand." Aarilina arched her eyes to the ground and then the ceiling while the feeling of such blood began to boil. Temptation to yell and scream was aggravating as well as the thought of being spoken to in second person was insulting. It wasn't the first time father treated Aarilina like a trophy and it wouldn't be the last. Princess Aarilinus was modest of such righteous beauty and title, but certainly was not arrogant or wicked like father. She slumpt in the chair, bored and tired, until the name Edward Bobbitt entered her innocent ears. Aarilina's eyes widened as the pupils dilated out while such limbs suddenly went numb. The feeling of a sharp dagger entered her shoulder blade as she shot halfway up with no words to speak of. "Sir Bobbitt did I not give you orders to watch my daughter with the most gracious care?" demanded the king. "Yes your highness, but she ordered me to engaged in a game so she would not be bored, sir!" "Ah I see," began King Owen as he looked around to all the knights, who were quiet and dared not to challenge him. The big man waited until the silence filled the room and with a sneer he spoke as though he were sucking the soldier's life force. It had been months since he had satisfaction to demonstrate the punishment for not carrying out his orders. For twenty years he would punish or destroy those who dared to rise against him. "Sir Jenkins when I give out my orders do I not expect them to be carried out thoroughly?" "Yes your highness, every order must be full filled with great importance," answered Sir Jenkins, the wisest of knights.

 The king gestured his closed mouth to the right side of his face while his eyes rolled to his daughter. The thought of a punishment was in store for the bodyguard. Should Sir Bobbitt be exiled or have his limbs torn apart by the Dark Wolves?

"Father it was I who betrayed your order, be merciful and spare Sir Bobbitt's life," answered the princess.

King Owen turned to the princess as her voice unleashed his ears with a plea for forgiveness. How would father decide a punishment or make a stand with his own blood when the princess had challenged his authority in front of all the knights. Aarilina was young, sweet, innocent and would plunge as queen if she endured incompetence from followers such as Sir Edward Bobbitt.

"I was unsatisfied and needed some excitement! Edward Bobbitt would not even look to tell me if he liked my dress until I ordered him." "What! He looked upon you!" exclaimed father as royal eyes widen and the thrust of his fist shivered the oak table. "Well yes father, I am a woman who desires the attraction from her faithful subjects what is there not to look at?" "Did you let him see your bosom?" "What is not to show? Every woman has them," smiled the princess. The king turned his wicked eyes away from Aarilina as he heard light snickers and chortles from the knights covering their mouths. What a disgrace and what could be done with this. "Cut Edward Bobbitt's eyes from out of his sockets and feed them to the pigs plus exile him from Aria. No, there is a better way! The Dark Wolves will be fed early this evening," sneered King Owen. "Guards take Mr. Bobbitt to the dungeons and feed him to the Dark Wolves!" "No father you can't do this! Please!" "Someday you will understand why I'm king, I can't allow our bodyguard to share to others what he has seen today. It will ruin your future as queen!" exclaimed King Owen as he gestured with the movement of his eyebrows.

The young, screaming, bodyguard was taken out of sight kicking and hitting, but remained captive under the restraints of the guards. Aarilina began to snivel, she felt responsible and captivated by the evil that had been bestowed upon the innocent bodyguard. How could this have been so obvious to believe that father would kill for the image held by a crown? Finally the servants arrived with golden platters of food as well as deserts of every delight. Everyone feasted their eyes upon the turkey legs, peas, carrots, potatoes and gravy. It seemed quite evident that the king was bewitched if he could still carry an appetite. The light flutter of butterflies filled the princess' stomach combined with nerves frozen in the flesh. "I lost my appetite?" she suspired and raised above the table to leave. "Where are you going?" demanded the king. "I'm going to my prison that you call the Mid Tower!" Without a word from father she made her leave with the echo of the closed door.

All the knights remained quiet, none took a bite from their plate and looked cautiously at the king as though it were poisoned. King Owen grinned while his mouth remained full and after the swallow of swine he reached for the goblet for the taste of wine. The last bit of potatoes tossed from one side of his mouth to the other. Suddenly the king's eyes panned left and right to the trust worthy knights as they stared at him with confusion. "Well?" began the king. "She decided to leave, but I'm still hungry," he chuckled while digging into his food. "Please eat, the food is getting cold," began King Owen as he watched the knights feast upon the food. King Owen turned to Sir Norcom with plans of his own. "Now we can get on to business! My daughter has plans to meet that peasant, Animus. Suitors from the five other kingdoms are entering the challenge of retrieving the mask to win my daughters hand in marriage." "Sir is that wise? What if the neighboring kingdoms find out our defenses and plan to invade Aria? We would be helpless to repel a surprise attack." replied Sir Norcom. "Not to worry I have already engaged a peace treaty with them and all is in good hands except my daughter's refusal." replied the king as he noticed the knight was getting worried. "She is planning to meet Animus in Humming Forest tomorrow night and I plan to have him thrown to the Dark Wolves. I command you to watch her and at the moment of deception she will be locked up in the High Tower." "As you wish," answered Sir Norcom as he took a bite from his plate and joined the other knights in celebration with the king.

Princess Aarilinus walked up the spiraling staircase thinking of the way father acted at dinner. A mind couldn't be more cluttered than a ball of yarn. With the twist of the door knob the feeling of home entered the body. She closed the door and walked to the dresser and pulled out her diary. While relaxed on the soft bed she opened the book to the sweet smell of perfume. It was nice and sweet, but suddenly became quite discouraging when the letter was found in the back of the pages instead of the front. With great suspicion Aarilina's eyebrows protruded with the slow grip of the folded piece of paper.

She raised its texture to her eyes, unfolded it to feel a mirror of love splash upon her very soul. The sight of Animus filled her imagination and she cracked a grin with the close of such eyes. Aarilina closed them after blowing the candle light, hoping for wonderful dreams of Animus.

The next morning arrived and the letter was delivered to Animus that very day. Aarilina occupied the morning by walking through the castle garden and the corridors of the stronghold. She played endless games of hide and go seek with the children of the noble families. It was mid-afternoon as Aarilina watched the clouds veil the sun as she suddenly slept on the grass. There was very little to do and the children were picked up by their parents.

The day went so fast and suddenly it became so slow to the hour of dusk.

An idea came to pass, with the visit to the library to choose a book; a book of her imagination would full fill the needs of this starving child. After visiting the library, the princess began having an unsettling feeling she was being watched. The eyes on the paintings sent shivers up and down her spine. The princess knew something was wrong when it seemed that she was being watched. After checking out two poetry books she left the library. The light chirps and scuff sounds were heard behind the walls as she continued to walk through the halls. She tried to hide the trembling in her legs, but found it difficult to pretend nothing was wrong. The anxiety kept teasing the princess' life long intuition and made her feel very scared. The paintings along the walls watched with every movement she made. The princess watched the paintings move their eyes through the corner of her left eye. The monarch could feel the goose bumps dance on her shoulders and suddenly began walking faster as soon as she saw something run from behind her in the distance of the corridor. Aarilina turned around, only to find nothing was there and felt her heart thumping from within her chest. Her skin began perspiring with trembling lips while Aarilinus took deep breaths as such mind went chaotic. Vibrations picked up a set of footsteps in the distance, behind the walls, and it made strange noises of a beast. She could already feel the beast sink its jaws into her flesh and tear her apart. The princess lost control and ran with the two library books in each hand. She made an abrupt turn to the next hallway and let out a terrified scream. Aarilina's out burst came as a surprise to the group of marching knights. They looked at Princess Aarilina confused, puzzled and wondered what they could do to assist her needs. Her eyes and mouth remained wide open as the trembling body suddenly relaxed. Never before had she felt so much anxiety other than the horrific childhood disasters of nightmares. "Are you ok your highness?" asked Sir Anson. "Yes I'm fine I just wanted to see how quickly I could get your attention." Aarilina wiped the sweat from her forehead while calming down and looked in their eyes. It seemed quite clear that the knights weren't fooled by the white lie. The princess would have to think of something else to encourage them that she would be alright. "Do you want us to walk you to your room?" asked Sir Jenkins. "No that's ok I can do it myself," she grimaced a fragile smile to the young knight. "We insist that we must protect our princess. Even if it may be nothing, we stand before you!" replied the leader of the knights, Sir Voles. He grinned and the group of marching knights kneeled before her. It seemed quite clear to the princess how they fell victim to such splendor and there for wanted to be guided back to her room. "Well thank you kind sir," she grinned as the knight held her hand and led the way.

    The knight and the princess were high in the Mid-Tower, Princess Aarilinus' room. She looked into the knight's eyes to say good- by to Sir Voles and wished that he could hear her pain. "Good night your highness," replied the knight as he nodded and left. The princess entered her room and crashed on her bed and instantly went to sleep. Hopefully this dream would be a pleasant one. As the sunset before the Mid-Tower Aarilina slowly closed her eyes and felt herself adrift from the rest of the body.

Aarilina opened her eyes after hearing the sound of cries outside the window. She slid out of bed and came to the window only to find it had iron bars on it. The sky was red and the kingdom was in ruin with the smell of rotting bodies.

With cold hands the princess clasped its coldness and metal exterior as she felt the sobs emerge from her soul. The feeling of being trapped in a room consumed the princess. The royal eyes looked upon the full moon and to the fires lit upon the land, the Outer and Inner gate were forged open. The setting of the sun split the sky into shades of blood that looked rubbed from one side to the other. Princess Aarilinus turned around to the door and saw father standing before her. It was the king only he was burned. "Father what happened to you?" Aarilina could feel the tears run down her cheeks. "You did this to me. You fell in love with that foolish farm boy and it cost me my crown! Aria has been destroyed because you married that peasant." "Father please, don't" her trembling lips struggled with the sight of him raising a dagger. The princess' heart began thumping hard as tears spilled from such eyes with a body trembling like a little bird. "Now you are going to die," his voice bellowed as the trembling eyes dowsed such hate with the tears that fell. Before the king could make a strike, a giant hand smashed through the barred window and gently took hold of the girl. Princess Aarilinus embraced the serenity of love surrounding her. After all was well the hand opened up and she was revealed to a giant wearing a mask. She looked below to see how small the buildings and people were as he took each step. Suddenly they appeared in a forest with the sound of water dripping into a creek without end. It was night and Aarilina walked around the ground after being released. She looked up at the masked figure and wondered who he was.

The giant suddenly shrank and looked down to her with its long beautiful, black, hair and black armor. As the figure shrank parts of his body unveiled, leaving his mighty arms and hands bare. "Who are you!" she demanded. "Furrengee," The voice echoed deeply through her ears and slowly she opened her eyes. The warmth of the sun shined through the window and filled her body with life.

It was only a dream or was it a message from god. The princess felt compelled to meet Animus and share the dream with him. Now that the inspiration of the mask made sense to what father boasted so triumphantly about. Aarilina got dressed, with great haste, for she had to learn more about this power. The princess stared out the window to see it was dusk and the sun was setting. It would be time to begin packing clothes and jewelry for Humming Forest.

The fields were nearly harvested and with the extra help from Sydney as well as all the siblings they would surely be finished by nightfall. A deliverer had entered Adam's field on horseback and trotted to correspond with them. The rider was dressed in silver armor and rode a black stallion. Animus was busy working the land with his three brothers Sydney, Gabriel and Aryan. Jada was hidden in the wagon of hay next to her brothers and was listening to their conversation. As brothers fight over what chorus they would also fight over who was right and who was wrong. "If I was king I would have seven wives so that every day would be a new beginning!" replied Sydney. "Yes, but how would you get anything done?" asked Aryan. "He wouldn't, we would be better off with the tyrant we presently have as king," replied Gabriel. "You are so demented!" replied Jada as she suddenly looked upon her brothers and jumped out of the wagon. "Don't you know that it's rude to listen in on conversations?" said Aryan. "Yes I know, but you guys do the same thing when I talk to mom about my problems. Now we're even." "Were you raised in a barn?" asked Sydney. "I was raised in a house-" Just then Jada looked up to the man in the silver armor. "I'm here to deliver a message for a young man by the name of Animus," answered the man as he pulled off his silver helmet to reveal his brown, hazel, eyes that glared upon the peasants from the night mare. He looked at all the faces and finally one of them stepped out to greet him. With a dirty, sweaty, face Animus acknowledged and held out his hand. "I am Animus"

The deliverer handed the letter to him and turned around on his horse to take off. Jada watched the stranger disappear into the distance and realized there was something weird going on. Adam walked from behind the wagon to see that everyone was taking a break. Aryan and Gabriel returned to work as Animus opened up the letter to unravel its mystery. It carried a perfume that smelled like the woman of his dreams and his heart began to quicken. Animus' face began to crack open as he read it silently. Sydney looked at Adam with a very puzzled look of disgust that was neither jealousy or excitement upon his brother's life. "Who is it Animus?" asked Adam curiously. "It's a letter from Aarilina. She wants to meet me at Humming Forest. Father I have to go! She could be in trouble!" "Animus your forgetting that your exiled from Aria!" "Trust me!" answered Animus as he ran to wash up at the house.

Dear Animus, My love,

I want to see you and long to be in your arms. I miss your gentle fingers caressing my lips and body. Every time you touch me it sets my heart on fire and I can't ignore it. I think about you constantly and can never get you out of my mind.

I think father has someone watching me. Every where I go I'm compelled to turn around to see who it is. Every time I do, there is nobody there. He has threaten to put bars on my window if he finds you, but that won't stop me from seeking you. He hopes to keep us apart, but it only makes me want you even more. My father is a fool and does not know what love is, why can't he let us be together?

The only way I can see you is if I leave tonight. Meet me in Humming Forest. Please be careful! Father won't hesitate to put you to your death and keep me a prisoner in my own heart.

love,
Aarilina

It was near dusk and Animus walked around Humming Forest, endlessly, to find the princess, but did not see her. The shadows along the branches and lower stumps were eerie. Animus could feel the anxiety fill the ice, cold, veins as a light tingly feeling bounced up and down his spine. The boy turned his head back and forth after hearing the hoot of the owl. The chirps of the robins and sparrows whistled a warning of the trap. He remembered that this was the very spot they first met. Suddenly a giant net was unleashed upon him and the farm boy found himself captured by the king's men. "Look at what we found," grinned one of the knights looking down at Animus. "It looks like we have got a trespasser," laughed another. "I'm not a trespasser I'm the princess' lover!" exclaimed the young man. "Lover huh." They answered as they began hitting and kicking him. "We'll see if she likes you when we demolish your face and cripple you. The princess won't like anyone who is deformed."

Animus could feel sharp thrusts in the face and stomach while the back of his head cracked with the strike of something hard. He could feel blood spill all over his face and the feeling of an electric current shot up his spine. The boy's vision grew dark as his ears went ringing with the feeling of being dragged by his legs. The soldiers marched back to the castle to show King Owen what they had captured.

As dusk drew near for the kingdom of Aria the princess was busy making preparations. The princess packed up her clothes, perfume, and jewelry in a bundle where she dreamed of the night to come where they would make sweet, passionate, love. When all was finished, she ran to open the door and came face to face with fear that it made her heart melt. "Father!" Aarilina stuttered to the abrupt appearance. "I was just coming to see you," lied the princess with a last minute thought. "If you were coming down to see me why would you need this?" he replied referring to the small baggage. Before the princess could come up with an excuse to why she was leaving. The king pierced the fright with an evil sneer and his eyes closed halfway. The princess searched father's facial expression for any sign of mercy, but only felt deception. "The letter I wrote in my diary-" "I have read it and I must say it is a disgrace to me and the kingdom. For you to fall in love with the peasant boy. I have been a very honorable father and hold you high above a place of gold." "A place of gold, is that all you care about?" cried Aarilina as tears began to well in her eyes. "This image of a beautiful queen holding a sword and shield, to be wise, stern and bestow justice through out the land!" declared Princess Aarilinus. "You couldn't be more wrong!" cracked King Owen as his eyes sparkled into hers. "Rules upon image that's all that matters to you! I shatter your image into a million pieces. I give up my sword and shield for any war. I will ensure peace and laughter for the world. I would enforce it by living the same way as my subjects, a slow and agonizing life of a peasant. I would deceive you just to escape into an adventure with Animus!" There was the dead of silence as the princess felt her heart ach and looked into his eyes. "Father, it is only love, what is the harm in that?" her voice echoed the words of her mother.

"The harm is him! The bloodline of my sworn enemy will rule the kingdom as the thought of his impure blood sickens me. The mere sight of a peasant ruling will destroy me, the royal family, and will leave me in disgrace!" "Is that all you care about? The heart of yours rather than the heart of mine?" The princess' voice was shaken in tears with eyes that remained unblinked as well as emotion unveiled like a broken glass. The king was quiet, too quiet, and this scared the princess. "I was hoping it wouldn't come to this. I have no other alternative, but to kill Animus and lock you in the High Tower." "You have captured Animus?" "Yes I have and to prove it I will let you see him. I will let him live if you choose to marry who I tell you to marry?" "You can't do that!" Her cries passed dispersing the air like water. "I can daughter and I will! Decide what you will do to prevent this terrible catastrophe and I will let Animus go, after you marry another." "There is no proof that you will keep your word is there?" "You will just have to trust me." "Trust! You don't know the meaning of the word trust, father. Trusting you is like reaching my hand through the mouth of a tiger." "Then I will show you how honorable I am by revealing Animus. Is that not trust worthy enough?" "No! Releasing him is trusting that you won't kill him." "You give me little choice princess, but I will let you speak to him. I will set him free only if you promise to end your relationship and by doing so you must tell him you don't love him. Humiliate him and tell him you don't want to see him again," replied the king. Aarilina dried her eyes with a sniffle, picked up her hooded cloak and followed father down the stairs to the dungeons.

King Owen and Princess Aarilinus tiptoed down to the dungeon followed by five knights. It was dark, wet and because of the harsh coldness Aarilina snugged deep into her cloak to keep warm. Prisoners, faceless, nameless, both men and women grouped up to the cells like scurrying animals, begging for forgiveness. The princess walked past them and felt their stares as well as their pleads. "Princess please help us!" they cried. "Your highness help me I implore you I have not stolen anything!"

Their sad eyes and dirty faces dominated the young girl's spirit. How could they be refused to live a quality life for petty crimes rather than locked up for life? Father ordered them to be silent and watched the knights hit them with wooden sticks as though they were dogs. Tears filled her eyes as she put it upon herself to ignore them in order to speak with Animus. They reached another chamber and the king unlocked the gate to enter a long corridor of cells. They walked past compartment with fewer inmates, this time they sneered at the princess like a piece of meat. "Hey baby want to have some fun," sneered an old feeble man from across the cell. "Your the one who did this to me," yelled another. Aarilina looked to see it was a much younger man who was angry and stuttered in each syllable. His face was dirty as eyes of a mad man glared at her like evil incarnate. Goosebumps covered her arms as the cool draft ran against the princess through the path.

Finally they reached the cell where the sad, young, man loomed alone and distraught. Aarilina could hardly believe that she was seeing Animus alive with such a distressed attitude before breaking his heart. It was days since they kissed and it would be the last time her eyes would grieve to break his heart. "Aarilina!" Animus shot up from the floor and suddenly realized he was restrained by old, rusted, chains. The peasant's eyes looked into the love of his life and suddenly felt very cold. His bruised face and dried blood revealed a battered farm boy, but that was far from a broken heart. Animus read it on Aarilina's face as well as feeling his blood drain from the bottom. Something was wrong, he couldn't believe he was getting the same feeling of shame from the king and the princess. "Why are you looking at me like I'm some criminal?" "Animus I've found someone else that falls in my heart's desire, I never loved you. You were nothing, but a resolute, a play-pretty of my amusement. I want you to disappear and never show your face again!" "But. . . " cried

Animus as his lips trembled and tears trailed down such cheeks as he felt the darkness unfold upon him.

There was no point in fighting it, he felt captured and had. Before another word could be spoken the princess left and so did four of the knights. King Owen opened the cell and walked in like nothing was wrong. The evil sneer on his face seemed to stick for all time as well as the cold expression of the knight. "You see, I always win and you will always be the foolish peasant." "Those are mighty words you use for a spoiled child?" The words ripped through the king like a blade. "What do you mean?" "A man so powerful such as you can't even cure the happiness in your own daughter." "You think you make my daughter happy? She spits on your nameless face!" "You probably told Aarilina to act this way. My father was right about you. You can't even help yourself, after your wife died you have been cursed as a short sighted freak of nature, a black shroud in every courtship. Why do you think you've not married after the death of the queen? Because you're envious beyond repair as well as everyone else's happiness is buried under your suffering and misery." "SILENCE!" exclaimed King Ruke Owen as the past memories emerged. "Throw the boy to the Dark Wolves!" he answered slowly in a deep voice.

Animus' heart stopped as eyes widened he could already feel his limbs begin to break apart. The feeling of teeth imbedded like razors made him quiver like a bird. Without another word Animus saw the knight pull a lever and felt himself give way to the thrust of air into the abyss of darkness. Animus felt the rush of air attack his cheeks while hearing the screams of wind brush upon his ears. Seconds passed as Animus finally hit the ground and raised his head with the sound of drumming in his ears. After minutes seemed like long hours Animus raised his battered body from the sand. The boy turned his blue eyes from side to side as the stinging emerged in his forehead. Had he broken his nose? No his knees and elbows broke the fall to the sand. The young man looked around to see there were dozens of torches that lit the aged, dusty chamber of bones and bricks. He grabbed a torch from the wall to wave it aside to see the huge number of skeletons that covered the sand. If there was a way to escape Animus would find it.

The King's Retribution

A strange flapping sound was heard and Animus turned around from facing the wall to discover five hideous creatures staring at him. They were larger than dogs and spread their pair of wings through the air like geese. Their hypnotic, red, eyes filled him with fear as the feeling of his knee caps shivered.

"Please don't eat me!" "Eat you," answered one of the beasts. "Yes you are the Dark Wolves are you not?" "Yes we are," spoke the leader. "Then what are you waiting for!" exclaimed Animus. "This boy wants us to eat him," chuckled another beast. "We eat only the ones who fear us. This one does not fear us," replied the leader as it continued to stare at Animus. "Tell me your name, boy?" "Animus. Animus Brokenheart." "Animus the king?" asked another. "No just Animus. Now you tell me your names!" "We do not answer to demands, little boy!" growled the leader. "Tell him our names. For all we know he probably is the one who will free us." "Shut up Shepherd or I will have you thrown out of the circle," barked the leader as he turned his attention back to Animus. "Very well boy, today is your lucky day I will tell you my name, but only if you tell us why you are here with us?" "I'm in love with the princess, I was thrown down here against my will and have been challenged to win her heart by retrieving the mask." "Mask you say," murmured a voice in the back ground. "He's the one who will free us, we must help him only then will the spell be broken," mumbled another. "Shut up!" bellowed the leader. "Who are you?" demanded Animus. "I am Rampant, The Black Sorcerer of Fire and Darkness," began Rampant and he gestured the other Dark Wolves to introduce themselves. "I am Earman, The Blue Sorcerer of Air and Sound." "I am Lore, The Silver Sorcerer of Water and Stone." "I am Shepherd, The White Sorcerer of Trees and Light." I am Malice, The Gold Sorcerer of Soul and Possession." The Dark Wolves grinned at Animus as they crept closer poking their red eyes at the young farm boy. What did they want? Who were they and why were they imprisoned in such a dark place, Animus thought to himself. Rampant walked towards Animus and studied him well, with the use of his nose. It was soon determined that Animus was to be untouched. "You are on a quest to retrieve the Mask of Furrengee. You have to promise us that you will set us free." "What if I refuse?" "Well if you do and we escape I will personally make your body a banquet for all of us." "Why don't you just fly out of here?" "If we did that do you think I would be standing here talking to you?" "We were put under a spell by a master of evil. Our hideousness would never be repented unless our captor set us free by wearing the mask," replied Earman. "How long have you been imprisoned like this?" "Ten thousand years ago we were the rulers of the first six kingdoms and we were brought down by deception. An evil wizard imprisoned us in the form of freaks until the time predicted for our release, a man by the name of Animus. This man, as king, would set us free to unite the kingdoms and bring peace as well as prosperity to the world." "That sounds very intense! How do you know that this person is me?" "Because it has been predicted for ten thousand years and there is order for every prophecy given to the insight of every sorcerer," answered Malice. "Don't you see if we leave the abyss our true form will return as it was thousands of years ago, permanently!" exclaimed Lore. "Who was the wizard that imprisoned you?" "I don't know his name," answered Rampant. "He was child like, with the appearance of a woman and the body of a man. He was tall and bold with silver streaks that ran through his hair like the color of the sun." "What was his name?"

    The Dark Wolves looked at each other before speaking and shook their heads. Something didn't seem to make sense with the reason why these sorcerers were imprisoned here. Was their a reason to feel pity for these five men to prevail in the common good, once their release was overcome. "It was a wizard named Xaggess who put us in this hideous form!" exclaimed Shepherd. "What has this got to do with me? I'm here to win Princess Aarilnus' heart." "Win her heart you shall when you set us free. It has been foreseen in the prophecy that you stand with us to unite the kingdoms and end the wars forever," grinned Malice. "With our help you could be the most powerful king in the land and no adversary will dare oppose you," cracked Rampant. "I don't know if putting pressure and intimidation on the neighboring kingdoms is such a good idea." "It's the most perfect idea! We could teach you our power and help you become a sorcerer. You would be invincible and capable of doing so much good as we had. It is your destiny to set us free and take your place as king of Aria," declared Lore. "I don't believe I will need your help after I retrieve the mask. It will enable me to be the king that Aria has needed. I will always be the man that Aarilina sees before her and have no desire for such power." Animus cracked a grin. "The mask will not give you all the power that we will bestow upon you young lord," replied Earman. "Yes. Imagine having control over the weak minds of man to unite the land against the rise of evil," continued Malice. "As well as the power to control night and day," persuaded Rampant. "It sounds tempting, but I think that the minds of man should remain free to make up their own minds. The control of night and day should remain in the control of Mother Nature." "Will you set us free?" growled shepherd. "I can't set you free if I'm confined to a dark prison with no way out." "There is a way out," barked Rampant as he nudged his head up to an opening. "There is a window near the dropped door where the king unloads his victims for us to feed upon. Our last victim by the name of Edward Bobbitt was sweet and tasty," cracked Malice as Animus looked at the beast with disgust. "A window? Is it barred?" asked Animus. "The bars are bent enough for a young man to fit through," answered Rampant. "How do I get up there?" asked Animus as he lifted his head up to see the bluish glow of light shine through. "We will lift you up and fly you there, but before we do that you must promise to free us," ordered Rampant. "After I have recovered the mask and rescued my beloved Aarilina I will free you for sparing my life. I do not ask anything from you except your silence to live your own life without involving yourselves in humanity," replied Animus. "Agreed," answered all five Dark Wolves at once. "Climb on my back and I will help you reach the exit," ordered the leader.

 Animus slid on the beast's back and felt its soft fur as well as the black, leathery, wings that began to spread open. The other Dark Wolves fluttered as well and helped their leader lift the farm boy in the air. While ascending in the air, Animus pondered at the idea of who these creatures were and wondered if setting them free was the best idea.

 Animus turned around to sprint through the trees and brush just as a miracle answered his call, the boy halted before a grazing horse. Without word or thought the boy felt his body jump and slide over the horse's back. The horse gruffed and snarled as they both charged through the open gates. The guards recognized Animus, but could not shut the draw bridges quick enough. The young man and the horse cascaded under the metal grate with great speed. He heard the metal hit the ground with a big thud and was happy that they escaped.

The sun anticipated dusk's resolution and bleached the sky reddish orange until the last tip disappeared in the horizon. Animus felt the wind hit his face and watched it thrust leaves as well as brush before his feet. The peasant unfolded the map and looked upon it, while daring to raise his eyes upon the face of the mountain. The temple was timeless, forged with rock and stone, unfolding in and out as a huge, triangular, pyramid. It rested inside of a mountain that had survived many wars and served as a hiding place for pirates.

Anxiety filled the boy's veins as the sight of the mountain face stared at him with evil. Animus looked at the entries written by his father, which revealed the mountain devoured young warriors who entered. The elders spoke of Shadow Mountain as a place where goblins stole little children and performed sacrifices. The haunting thoughts of dought entered the boy's mind: *How could he dare retrieve a power for love when all danger vowed against him?* Animus turned around to the horse that had helped him escape and knew what had to be done. "I wish you could go where I'm going friend, but if I never return you should be free to roam where ever you choose," replied Animus as he pet the horse's mane.

The horse nudged its head into Animus' face and gruffed a racket just as the young boy began to grimace a grin. The peasant quickly gave the horse a quick nudge with his hand and watched it run in the distance. For a long time Animus watched the sun set and wondered if he would ever see the sun again.

After minutes of thought Animus began the passage to the mouth of Shadow Mountain. He raised his dead heart from a kneeling position and glared upon the mountain face. Every step of the way the feeling of anxiety brought its toll upon such mind as the imagination of a dragon bursting out to attack him seemed to keep him on his toes. Animus stepped through the long corridor like cave to the sight of the temple that stood in its center with no light except what came through the eyes of the mountain. After a short trot, Animus halted at its massive size in comparison to any castle and slowly touched the rough brick wall while looking at the map. The secret lever to open the back door was very near to grasp. Suddenly, the farm boy felt a weak impression in the brick wall and pushed it in. A small crack in the wall was revealed.

Animus walked in the tunnel and felt the intense humidity as though he were inside a volcano, the sound of bats made their path with squeals. It was dark, stale and a long corridor of torches filled the long spaces. Animus could barely see anything in the gloom of fog and darkness. The intimidating sight of skeletons and statues holding torches held Animus' soul captive. The immense space of darkness in between each sight of torches, burning, in the darkness made Animus wonder how old the temple was. It appeared that Adam, his father, was right about the fortification of what laid in store for the challenger. Animus walked through the darkness to grip the first torch and suddenly turned around after hearing a grinding noise from behind. He turned, waiving the torch around to see the secret passage door closing.

The grinding bestowed an echo to the young man's ears chanting the words welcome to your death. Sweat perspired from the boy's forehead as he turned and began walking down the corridor. While making each step the peasant thought of less intimidating things. Flashbacks entered the farmer's mind of Aarilina, her long hair, luscious lips and dreamy eyes. The dream about their wedding was just in his grasp except that's all it was, a dream. If he was to prove such valor and honor to Princess Aarilinus he would have to use every once of agility to possess the mask.

Animus took a deep breath and wiped the sweat from his forehead. It was obvious that the other suitors who entered from the front entrance would remain trapped as well, but would not survive the setting of the traps. Animus drew his hand up and curled the locks over such ears to open the folded piece of paper. The eyes of an adventurer focused for anything unexpected while walking through the straight and narrow corridor. The sound of water dripping from the ceiling was the constant reminder of the sweat from his own body. The drops entered the ears, which invited a great deal of annoyance to the peasant. Animus raised his eyes and head over the map, containing a maze of tunnels marked with blood, marking all the traps in the citadel. The feeling of hopelessness engulfed the mind as Animus' eyes touched the path and realized that he missed something. The map revealed there was a cross road up ahead, but his eyes prevailed to say that the tunnel was going straight, infinitely. Suddenly, the boy walked straight into a glass barrier that bestowed pain upon his head.

Animus took a moment to rest from the unexpected blow and made sure that he wasn't bleeding from his nose. The farm boy turned his attention to the map and found the thick, hollow, line crossing over the path. Animus would have to retrace the steps to the chamber of the mask. The young man's eyes glared at the dwindling flame of the torch and knew that surviving included seeing where he was going. The boy ripped his old, wool, overcoat given to him by his grandfather to feed the fire of the torch. With such grace in his fingers, he wrapped it around the torch and watched the fire grow. The torch lit brighter as Animus swung it around the dark.

Animus found a staircase going down and looked at the map to see that it was right on target, leading through a tunnel to an open corridor. Excitement filled the boy's heart, which made him feel convinced that the mask was in that corridor and that retrieving it would be easier than imagined. Without a second thought he ran down the set of stairs, which was dirty and the floor was sweaty. Each spider web passing the corner of his eyes managed to get bigger with each thrust of his leg. Every step of the way, Animus held the map close to his heart and focused on the slippery climb down. The farm boy walked through the giant spider webs and heard the sound of giant mouse traps unleash themselves to the tip of his quick, animated, feet.

Animus stopped and waived the torch to see the skeleton remains of animals the size of sheep dogs. With a raised arm to his brow, the peasant lowered the torch towards the ground to find there were dozens of spikes that would pierce the ground and then lower themselves below ground. Animus continued his raised eyelids searching up, down and around the stretch of corridor. Suddenly something echoed in his ears with the sound of scuffing and the light whis-

The King's Retribution

tling sound in the darkness ahead of him. As well as the drip, drip sound of water falling from the ceiling. Animus swung his torch back and forth to see what was in front of him, suddenly he came across something startling. "Ohhh my god!" Animus' eyes widen as he saw rats the size of dogs creep up to him.

They quarked their heads while licking their lips and fangs as their beady eyes glared at the farm boy. They hissed at Animus and crept closer as the boy swung his torch to prevent himself from becoming dinner. One rat jumped at Animus to bite him, but was thrusted back by the burning fire of the torch. The rats smelled the burning of their comrade and scurried through holes in the walls.

After all was well, Animus continued the walk and found himself in a large room filled with boulders. Statues and a stream of fire endured itself on three ledges along the walls. The boy looked at the map after taking a few minutes to look around. He suddenly felt stricken with fear as the room was revealed to be an arena for a challenge. Animus wiped the sweat from his forehead and was happy that he wouldn't have to worry about giant rats. Now he would have to worry about a new fear making way to his direction. Animus picked up a long weird looking cloth that was clear and recognized it as snake skin.

Animus' fear was the feeling of being trapped with giant rats and the revelation occurred in the fear of what laid before him, which was a giant snake. He turned his eyes upon the warrior statues on the ledge and discovered each of them held a weapon that could easily be taken from their grip. The reflection of a silver sword signaled a returned SOS like the morning star, javelin, and shield.

Animus traced his eyes upon the map to see a small note that a secret door would open with the recite of a lever and the Libra was to prevent him from going any further. Through the entrance would be another chamber to endure a new challenge. The farm boy's eyes looked up from the map to the choking sight of something large, sliding its way out a giant hole. Animus felt the goose bumps cover his arms in place of fire and death as he folded the map slowly. With a quick leap to a boulder he witnessed the beast slithering along the sand. It looked as though the snake was more interested in the giant rats that were trapped in the chamber. Quickly Animus dropped the torch the ground and ran to the statue holding the silver sword. He watched the Libra hiss and snarl at the rats before it lunged its fist like head to one of four rats.

He took advantage of the distraction. He ran to the statues holding the shield, javelin, morning star and slid them inside his leather belt. He turned around to see the Libra stuffing its mouth with rats. Suddenly, its head turned to face Animus and licked its lips as it spiraled towards him. Animus could feel the ivory sabers and yellow eyes embed themselves into his body. He closed his eyes and reopened them, hoping deep in the heart that a man's life would be spared.

The peasant saw the statue pointing its bow loaded with an arrow to the key hole. The arrow was made of silver with white feathers covering the rear. Without a thought the Libra charged the young man with its sharp slithers around the huge rocks and climbed up the boulder with its neck. Animus' heart began to race as drops of sweat perspired from his face. He heard it snarl as well as the sight snapping jaws, revealing the shiny sabers. He would have to come back for the bow and arrows.

With great speed the peasant leaped off the ledge and onto the sand as the Libra lunged its head, but grasped empty air. The rich stench of death unleashed itself from the snake's mouth in the form of venom spilling upon the boulder. Animus lured himself in a series of laps around the chamber knowing that the snake could pick up his scent, but it would not pin point his location. With the stroke of his hand and strides, he picked up the lit torch from the dirt. He quickly slid in the cavity of one of the boulders. Animus watched through the small slits to the outside space of the impending danger that waited. He watched the Libra slither fast and well upon all four corners of the chamber until it disappeared behind a large boulder in the distance. Animus unfolded the map to see if his father wrote any clues to escape. Sweat bombarded his face as such lips trembled with fear, he needed time to find the lever. Then it came to him, the key hole was the target of the statue holding the bow and arrow. Yes, that was the way to escape the clutches of the wicked Libra and proceed with this monstrous quest. Spiders the size of a large man's fist blocked his path and he burned them with the torch.

Animus took a deep breath and slowly crept outside the crevice of the boulder and looked around. All was silent as chills filled his spine as well as his ears ringing. Animus felt the dryness in the back of his throat and needed some water. There was nothing to suggest that the Libra was here, but there was also nothing to assure that the beast had given up. Obviously it was looking for dessert and would not retire until the boy was deep in its belly. Animus walked to the middle of the chamber while keeping his eyes peeled for the giant snake. He could see the key hole in the corner of his eyes as well as the statue pointing to it with the weapon needed to open the gate. Animus felt no fear and sensed the opportunity to seize the bow and arrow to open the access for the next chamber.

With an abrupt trot, he charged towards the boulder to make the climb to the top of the giant rock. Suddenly his blood stopped to the sight of death. Animus' eyes glared wide open as the hooded Libra rose its head up with its golden hooked eyes aloof into Animus' eyes. It let out a sneer with the snap of its death trap unleashing a stream of poison. The farm boy raised his shield as he heard the sound of burning and crackling upon the surface. With its poisonous venom it lunged its head up and griped the metal exterior of the shield. Animus shrieked in fear as he bestowed the Libra with such a blow from his morning star and pulled out his sword. With the powerful thrust of the blade he punctured the beast near its mouth. The peasant felt himself thrown through the air from the top of the boulder and kept his shield in front of him as much as possible. The snake let out a scowl as globs of venom shot in Animus' direction and struck the shield leaving more burns. Animus' eyes poked out from the side of the shield to watch it slither over the boulder. The Libra spiraled with its long wicked body to approach the one that had become the challenge.

Animus rolled his exhausted body along the white sand and jumped to his feet after the Libra spit its last venom. He looked upon the damage done to the shield and realized the silver sword was imbedded in the snake's neck. Animus could hardly believe how lucky he was, but felt deep inside that he was pure of heart. The fighting was merely survival and whatever limits of doom laid, there would always be a way. Animus gripped the morning star with its long chain and ball filled with sharp ridges. He tore out from the sands like a rabbit and felt the heat of the Libra slither its long body in his direction. Animus had to get to the silver arrows before the snake would have the chance to take a bite out of him.

The farm boy jumped up to the square like boulder and swung his body up to the ledge. Animus swung the silver shield on his back as his eyes enchanted the statue with the silver arrows. Just as the young man counted the tenth arrow he pulled one out to load in his bow. His eyes stared dead at the Libra, while it spiraled its body on the boulder and raised its hood to him. Its tongue went in and out as Animus dipped the arrow into the stream of fire from the ledge and pulled it out to aim at the beast. The fire turned silver with each streak of the flame raising in ribbons and with the pulsing of his biceps Animus drew his wrist back. His eyes trembled with the reflection of the Libra's raised jaw as he slowly let go of the string and grip of the arrow. He heard the squeals of pain unleash themselves in the room as he watched the arrow shoot into its mouth. The arrow imbedded itself inside the snake's throat and silver fire engulfed the exterior of its reptilian scales. Animus watched the head of the spiraled beast catch fire as flames shot from its open jaws. Animus dodged the inferno as the snake went into convulsions and soon its head exploded like the sound of thunder. The Libra collapsed to the sand and laid motionless while the fire fueled from its body.

A tear spilled from Animus' right eye with the haunting thought that he could have been killed. It was obvious that his fighting could only be imaginable with the frightening question of what if? How could he have come this far when all he had ever known was the harvest taught from father? It seemed possible that the only way he defeated the Libra was because it was fate. Animus jumped down from the ledge to retrieve the sword imbedded in the snake's neck. He walked closer to the corpse while covering his nose due to the stench of death that loomed the area. The young man dowsed the region of the sword with sand and pulled the silver handle from the flesh revealing the porcelain gleam of the blade.

Animus slid the sword into his belt and pulled rubble apart to reclaim the silver arrow lodged in its mouth. He returned the arrow to the sling and gripped the silver morning star as well as the javelin.

With a light touch upon the fierce weapons he felt eternal power. The morning star's handle was smooth and shined with the silver color like the javelin. There remained a mystery in these unimaginable weapons that were abandoned in this chamber. The peasant took one last look upon the sand that was a burial ground of lost warriors. After viewing the map his next challenge was the mask chamber, which sent chills upon his lower back. The young man pointed his bow to the key hole, as his hair raised on the back of his neck. With eyes so great he watched the arrow animate from his bow and spill into the key hole unveiling a door from underneath.

Animus felt with his fingers and endured the pain in his leg, which was like the feeling of a dagger stabbing him. He staggered in the darkness of shadows while the funnel of heated air spilled from the cracks below. The great evil that was near wouldn't stop him from thinking about Aarilina and continuing the journey. The mask surfaced as well as the good he would do with it. Anger filled the peasant's thoughts with what words King Owen said to him in the dungeon. The adrenaline rush filled his veins like boiling water. Suddenly the innocent voice of Aarilina whispered such sweetness as sugar sweetens such taste buds. The boy found a dead torch and raised it to the fire discharging from the hot lava shooting streams of fire near the peasant.

The stream of fire flourished from the angry lava, which lit Animus' torch and turned around realizing that the journey had to end with proclaiming the mask. The young man ran the torch left to right and discovered the tunnel straight ahead. The peasant's eyes pierced the darkness with the help of the torch. The rich aroma of corpse filled his lungs heavily and well as though nobody had gone any further.

Animus wiped his face from both the tears and the sweat that streamed upon his cheeks. He was locked in the temple from Princess Aarilinus, consumed with the fear of failing. How was he ever to see the light of day when he was vanquished inside a cave? He smelled death around him as he feared the worst of what had yet to come. Animus got up scratching the edge of his back against the gritty wall and felt something tickling his neck. The peasant jumped and shrieked as he knocked it off with his hand. Animus brushed his torch forward to view the mystery before him. It was a tarantula and it ran away from him in the shadows of the darkness. The farm boy lifted the torch around to see the skeletons and a long corridor ahead.

Animus kept taking each step slowly as he waved the torch around to be sure he wasn't going to be attacked. Suddenly a giant spider jumped out in front of Animus from the darkness. He pulled out the silver sword and swung with all his might to defend himself. The numerous eyes stared back at him and the spider charge after the young man with its giant pinchers. Animus began running back, but then turned around to burn the spider with the torch. It squealed in pain and scurried back into the darkness of the tunnel it came from.

He could feel the weakness in his knees tremble with fear. The hair on the back of Animus' neck began to stand on end. Animus anticipated more giant rats or spiders with a strange numbness in his ankles and felt the sharp teeth of rats eating him alive. After the long walk down the corridor of statues and skeletons he came forth to the entrance of another chamber. Animus opened the door and walked through to see the room was round. There was a catwalk made of silver, which filled his heart with enchantment as he saw the hidden treasure before him.

Animus' eyes widen as he saw the mask glowing on a pillow with a ray of light from the top suspending it in the air. He took a step forward and suddenly a large morning star swung out to hit him. Animus dodged it by swinging his body back and watched the spiked sphere return through a hidden passage way. Animus looked around the chamber and realized it was shaped like a hollow ball. He watched his new adversary swim below the hot lava below. It was a dark, red, serpent and before submerging itself back into the pool the serpent fired specks of fireballs from its mouth. Animus ducked and felt the rush of air sweep across his fore head. The creature dived back into the pool as Animus rose from the surface and waited for a moment of security. The farm boy was confused and frustrated. How was he going to get the mask when all these traps were preventing him from walking across the catwalk? Father said it would be easy, was he wrong? Animus opened the map again to see if there were any clues that would help him. His eyes drew near a poem written down. Animus raised his voice realizing it was not a poem at all, but a spell for safe passage and read it out loud.

Only one that is brave to walk across the bridge
must not only risk the hearts of others,
but his own and walk across the bridge
with his eyes closed for it is not the demons that are shown
but your reflection that have the traps rigged.

Animus hesitated before looking around the chamber, the words stuck into his head as well as the rest of the poem. The boy looked around the gold color exterior of the compartment and the silver color catwalk. He felt with his heart and saw one thing in common with all of them. They showed a reflection of him and realized that was what set the traps. Animus trusted himself and closed his eyes. Trusting absolute darkness, he took two steps upon the catwalk since he was known to be such a dreamer he put his heart to the test.

The boy's mind began to flutter to the times as a child crying from the fear of darkness. He was scared of the dark and needed someone to help guide him through the blindness. Then there was his father who helped him through it. *"Imagine yourself with nothing to fear in the dark and you will free yourself from the dark,"* replied Adam. *"I'm scared of the dark!" "Animus, the darkness can't hurt you only you can hurt yourself in the darkness."*

Animus imagined the catwalk and at the end of the silver walk would be Princess Aarilinus with her arms wide open. Her long eyelashes and brown eyes touching his, with such fine lips waiting to be embraced. She was wearing a yellow dress and calling his name. "Animus your almost here!" her voice enchanted his ears and gave him hope.

He could hear the bubbling sound of the lava pit below him and the strong sense of humidity that filled his forehead with sweat. Before he knew it he bumped into the soft pillow and opened his eyes. After enduring the sharp light from above, he slowly traced his fingers over the smooth textured metal. The maw was embossed with dark, marble, lips pushing upwards in a somber look of a warrior and the outside of the eyes were shaved smoothly along the cheeks as the nose stuck out abruptly.

Animus heard in moments the sound of voices as a child when playing with his brothers and sister. They were playing kings and thieves and the day seemed to trail on forever at the age of five. Animus cracked a grin when he experienced the goodness of past lovers who fought for the preservation of love. An image of Furrengee entered Animus' mind, which was foggy. He could see the warrior tower over him with a big grin and kneeled down to the farm boy at eye level. The warrior was described as clearly as his father had told them. His eyes were dark brown and his beautiful hair hung past his chest.

"You have been chosen Animus to use the mask," his voice was deep as well as strong and his eyes looked deep into Animus as though he had known him for a long time. "The people in your world need you. Someone who is brave, someone who has been there in the poor person stead. You must carry the torch and protect the people of Aria. You must stay pure for the power of good." "What if I fail?" asked Animus as he watched a grin appear on Furrengee. Suddenly Animus felt a wave of strength push upon him like nothing had before. A slight grimace endured upon his face as a surprise. "The fiduciaries and I shall be here to guide you." Animus never expected the day that he would meet Furrengee. "I will help the people of Aria, I promise," cried Animus as tears filled his eyes and took the warrior's big hand. As his hand gripped Furrengee's he looked up to his brown eyes matched with the tan skin and mighty, black armor. Animus never felt so much positive energy enter his body and he had never felt so important. With a nod from the giant, Animus watched Furrengee walk away in the mist of the white fog that surrounded them.

Animus opened his eyes to the simple touch of the mask and hoped that one day they would meet again. It was a day dream or was it a trans? The farm boy slowly removed the mask from the pillow and gently traced it over his face. The ray of light from above diminished as the mask illuminated the room. With the white light, shining so brightly the metamorphosis of Animus and Furrengee took place. His body became robust and muscular as his hair grew past his shoulders. Parts of his bangs grew past his eyes. The black, shiny, armor immerged out of the boy's skin as well as a black, flapping, leather cape that sank knee level. The memories of thousands emerged into Animus' mind as well as voices of the good granted the rights to mobilize his body to follow such heart. Animus turned to the cat walk and exited the chamber. He walked like he was on a mission in a steady beat to venture to an endless destination.

Deep in the depth of the temple the legend would be reborn. A power discovered and remained through his love and desire for one woman. A fist thrusted a hole through the temple as quick as lightning and as loud as thunder through the brick walls that blocked his path. He peered outside the hole to see the stars as well as the moon. He stood upright while his mask shined blue, his armor polished from the stars while his cape flapped in the wind. Slowly he leveraged his hand with the magical weapons found in the chamber. They laid upon the ground near the forest of Shadow Mountain and shined upon the moon. The moon was full among the dark, blue, sky. Suddenly with great will his body became larger. The boulder, from the mountain, was kicked out of his path with the proof that he was no longer weak as some had thought.

The princess continued to comb her hair while she soaked herself in the tub of hot water until it was soft and wet as could be. Jenna was busy helping Aarilina get ready for bed and knew that the High Tower was limited. She looked into the mirror, as the handmaiden combed her hair back, to look upon her gorgeousness. Her white skin reflected pure and her dark, brown, eyes were sad as she kept thinking in deep thought of her future. Jenna stopped what she was doing and left to have a group of handmaidens fetch more hot water. Aarilina rinsed her face with the water thinking about her attractiveness even more and knew if she was to be lost father would never be able to forgive himself. Aarilina's magnificence was a symbol to all the people that Aria is the beautiful nation and no escort could resist her.

The branches of the trees swayed down as if the wind took effect on them. Furrengee stepped over the brushwood and stood looking in the distance with the castle in his eyes as well as the kingdom before him. The animals ran in all directions, the mice and rabbits ran to take shelter into the ground or in the trees. The wolves and wildcats took refuge running away from the stranger. The giant took a step upon the old bridge made of wood and stone. It faltered apart in splinters of wood, sharp and deadly as well as the broken cement blocks that faltered in the water. Through depths of the cold, mucky, water, Furrengee gathered his strength to overpower the river and grew bigger as he lifted his foot out of the water.

    Her eyes were hazel brown, some thought they were dark brown, and viewed the attraction of herself to the mirrors that surrounded her. The servant returned with the ointment used for the princess fingernails. With the help of Jenna polishing her finger nails while bathing in the tub. Aarilina began thinking about her future without Animus. Would life be the same with out her other heart? "Jenna if you loved someone so much would you kill yourself to see him in the after life?" "Child what speak is that. In a matter of days you will become queen of the kingdom!" "Please answer the question. It's important," replied Aarilina as she closed her eyes. "Well I don't know he would have to mean more to me than life itself." That was all Aarilina needed to hear to make a decision about her future. After Jenna was finished polishing Aarilina's fingernails she helped the princess out of the tub and dried her well with a towel. "Leave me please. I want to be alone." There was a slight pause with Jenna who knew her mother well and obeyed Aarilina to give her some space. The princess' life wouldn't be the same, she would take her life before giving her heart away. Beside the soft touch of a hand caressed to the chin, her eyes did not blink for they welled up with tears of hopelessness. The princess slipped her nightgown on as she thought was this truly the end? Surely not. He would cascade through the doors and have her tepid and warm body fall into his. With the breath that would cast knights asleep in a single bound she blew a kiss goodnight to the candle light. It cast frenzied shadows along the walls of her room as she slid into the covers and snuggled into a bed that was not hers. She would dream of her soul mate and the adventures that would be explored.

    The overbearing giant stepped over the walls of the first gate which was heavily guarded. At night there was not that many guards since the guardians, archers and the hunters were resting. The guardians and a few knights ran out of their towers to defend the castle only to come to a surprise halt. They lowered their swords and axes while watching the giant walk past without even noticing them. After their shock came to an end it seemed sensible in their mind to attack while they still could. Furrengee looked down on them, they looked like ants that you see walking along the ground after the rain. In the deep subconscious of Furrengee was the revenge that he was looking for to step on them and crush them like bugs. Thoughts embraced through Furrengee of Animus as a child. It was revealed that the rich nobleman children picked on him for living a poor life as a peasant. Except this time it had to be ignored if he was to survive revenge and self greed. Other wise it would destroy him from getting to where he wanted to be.

The archers griped their bows and shot arrows that were poisoned. The arrows could not embed themselves into Furrengee's body; the powerful armor worn was made of something unimaginable. It looked like any other armor, only the mask granted its gift to be invincible to who ever wore it.

The few brave knights that were there tried to slay the giant, but failed. Furrengee walked on with his heart pumping for the woman he loved. Some of the warriors fled, those that got in the way were accidentally stepped on by Furrengee. The great warrior felt no pain or pity for those that inflicted pain upon him.

Aarilina was awake unable to sleep in the High Tower that was nothing more than a prison. Voices in her head chanted of disaster about Animus, kingdom, and life. Her wants and desires were jumbled and unfocused as she watched the chandelier move from the wind. Life was anticipated to a different viewpoint of an uncertain future. Would she live or die? The princess would marry no other except Animus who was deemed worthy. Aarilina made her mind up to the final end of a royal life. Her red lips trembled to the self dought that he was alive and if he wasn't she would die! It was arrogance that the king would disagree and fulfill the needs for her. It was what she feared more than anything in the past. Just the thought of being sad her whole life she perspired sweat through her cheeks as well as the shakes in such arms. The body was hot as though she had the flu. When closing her eyes images of father, who was burned alive, from the dream surfaced to scare her. She tried to keep hope that her paramour would come to the rescue.

All was not lost, for Furrengee had stepped over the second gate and was inside the castle grounds. The masked giant looked around through numerous towers many tall and small. Some were lit and full of life others were dead with the decayed scent of emptiness. He looked through the blocks and stone that were lit, none of them held her captive, until he looked up to the highest tower which was higher than he. Furrengee gathered all the strength there was and grew in size to match the height of the tower.

Aarilina woke up to the apprehension of the cool breeze drying her face. It pushed some of her long, black, hair back in peels and clumps, blowing into such a striking appearance. She rose out of bed while pulling her hair over her ears and looked at the window. It was wide open, inviting the cool breeze into her room. Her chilled naked body was like ice with every current wave of air. Aarilina felt her body tingle as though she was being watched. The brown eyes stared at the window with the white curtain and felt them reach out for her with invisible hands. Suddenly, something jerked the bars as well as broke the glass upon the wooden floor. The princess listened to the metal bars roll along the wooden floor. Her intuition revealed that the wind broke her window. Aarilina quietly tiptoed to the corner of her room where she was back against the wall. With every deep breath of anticipation goose bumps made their way to her skin. Princess Aarilinus had never felt so cold upon her limbs, but felt the cold sweat embrace her forehead. The monarch turned around peeking around the corner to see what there was to fear and saw the window curtain blowing in the wind. Then Aarilina's eyes grew wide after witnessing a giant eye looking at her.

Neutral and strong they revealed no love or hate, because it was a mask. The eyes of the person wearing the mask looked at the princess and melted with her. Through her chilling screams. Furrengee gently grabbed the princess with his hand and brought her out to see the trembling body and shiny eyes. Princess Aarilinus was scared at first, but felt a sense of love through its eyes and Furrengee felt it. As the masked giant walked away from the tower he closed the hand in a cup to protect the princess from harm. The archers, hunters, guardians and knights had regrouped with a plan to destroy the horror that invaded the king's castle. Furrengee cradled the princess carefully as though she was made of glass and did not want to loose her for anything. Every arrow was ignored and every spear thrown at him whether it hit him or missed was forgotten.

The dark stranger did not bother to return an attack of annoyance. The knights and guardians engaged the catapults with lit fireballs. The knights lit the loaded catapults with a torch and shot it at Furrengee.

The fireballs thrusted their way through the night with each crackle and scream while it collided into the middle of the giant's back. The masked giant turned to see where they came from and noticed the wicked contraptions shooting the fireballs at him.

With emotional eyes, Furrengee raised his right hand in front of his mouth and blew a slight whistle transpiring a curse upon the atrocious contraption. Aarilina held onto the masculine chest of the warrior while watching the battle carry over from the top of his hand. Furrengee continued the long journey to the first gate and saw the archers before him, shoot their arrow lit with fire. The arrows stuck deep into his chest as the giant wiped them off like clumps of food. A fireball cascaded through the air and hit the giant in the head. Furrengee turned around and held his hand out to catch all the fireballs. He folded his hand and crushed the orbs into diamonds and let them fall to distract the soldiers. The warrior turned around to make his final destination while the soldiers stopped in their tracks to gather the diamonds, to satisfy their greed.

Furrengee stepped over the brick wall of the first gate with each cascading vibration. The rabbits and squirrels ran away from the path to take cover in the trees. He was strong and powerful while walking through the woods like a diabolic machine. "Come on he's getting away," declared one of the knights to the greedy soldiers picking up the diamonds. He jumped to his armored steed loaded with every weapon imaginable. Other knights loaded another steaming, steely, ball into the catapult. The flickered light of fire streamed from their torch they cut it with the swiftness of their blade. Suddenly the steely exploded with a big boom, the sharp ringing in the knight's ears was not all that alarmed them. The whole catapult was on fire and so was the screaming knights running for the nearest cow bath.

Twenty fireballs flew through the air screaming their names until the giant came to an abrupt stop, turned around, thrusted his hands out and fired them back to the ground. Scattered chunks of blazes were blowing the catapult to pieces and defaced the knights.

In the eyes of the guardians and warriors, never had there been a power displayed like this. Battles that waged war have always been fought in an army in the thousands. What made this invasion different was not that a single person broke into the castle gates, but this person was a giant. The troubling questions that emerged from their minds was how could this be possible?

"Wake up the king! We've got an evil witch at work!" ordered Sir Seres as he turned his head to Sir Anson, who turned to find the king's advisor and guardian, Sir Bombardis. Sir Bombardis ran deep to the king's chamber and found him sound asleep. "Sir, the princess has been taken!" commanded Sir Bombardis as he lit some candles to wake up the king. "When was she taken?" demanded Ruke as he rubbed his eyes and tossed the blankets aside. King Owen enjoyed his royal sleep as always, but disliked anyone waking him up. This time it was different and King Owen jumped out of bed to change into his clothes.

"She was just taken now, your highness," replied Sir Bombardis. "Princess Aarilinus is the only living heir to the throne," murmured King Owen as he tried to think who would betray him. His gut feeling revealed to him that Animus was involved, but it was washed away when he remembered that the Dark Wolves would have ripped his body apart. The haunting question remained, who would dare challenge the king and on what grounds would war prevail? "Assemble the soldiers! Whether they like it or not we're going to get her back. Now!" he shouted as his face turned red. "Your highness the suitors already left to rescue the princess. The knights and archers left with them to slay the giant," informed the knight. "I will go with a small contingent to see that this is solved." The king swung his night cap off and watched it bounce off the wall, behind his bed. King Owen turned his head to the faithful guardian, Sir Bombardis, and raised his eyebrow. The advisor nodded as he panned his eyes from the

The King's Retribution

ground and back into the eyes of his king. "There is nothing to see! It towers the castle and it has no fear for the knights. It instigates the catapults to explode!" exclaimed the guardian as he turned around for the king to dress himself. "I must say your majesty, is it possible that the legend of Furrengee exists? That the power of love exists in a mask? Love so powerful that invincibility and desire exist as one?" "Yes those things are true, but I always thought of it as a legend." The king's lying lips muttered as his eyes looked to the wooden floor then to his knight. "How do we stop something invincible? We are no match for him!"

The king stopped what he was doing and felt that the guardian caught him in his tracks. King Owen buckled his pants and put a sweater on as he turned around to face the guardian while preparing to speak. It seemed clear that there was going to be some explaining about the mask. "The mask resolves around the feeling of pure love. With this power the deepest desire uses the mask's endowment to stop anything in its path. As long as the person wearing the mask did not inflict pain on the innocent, all would be well. If there was destruction or greed the guardians of the mask would curse the possessor. All adversaries attacking the possessor would perish in the bestow of a curse." "If the mask resolves around love, why did you send suitors to retrieve it from the temple?" "I wanted my daughter to marry somebody who could not only protect her, but broaden the road of wealth and royalty for the family. A long time ago I dreamed that the mask was real, but whenever I awoke, it seemed like nothing more than a fantasy. My wife passed away seventeen years ago, Aarilina's mother and queen to the throne. When I read that a single mask worn by anyone could bring a loved one back to life, I began sending knights to locate and retrieve it. The mask has unimaginable power to make people around you grow jealous and greedy that is why it is placed in the citadel." "How do you know so much about the mask and the citadel?" "I've read the legend since I was a child and have made it known by sharing it with others. Ten thousand years ago five sorcerers ruled the corrupted land until a warrior stood up to them and their great army. A rebellion was led by this giant to free mankind and the kingdoms forced to be united by these evil sorcerers. Legend entails that a rise of power, forged by

Furrengee, freed all men. A powerful wizard by the name of Xaggess joined the resistance and through war they breached the sorcerers, leaving them defeated. Furrengee and Xaggess exiled the sorcerers in an abyss concluding that with such wickedness they should never be aloud to escape. The balance of Ayana would be extinguished and life as we know it would be corrupted. It was written in prophecy that the king of Aria would set the Dark Wolves free and corruption would return in the bloodiest of wars." "But sir who would do such a thing?" "The Great Prophets predicted that King Animus would rule after a masked giant invades the castle grounds setting the sorcerers free." "But we do not have sorcerers in the abyss; we only have the Dark Wolves." "The Dark Wolves are the sorcerers you half wit!" "What happened to Furrengee and Xaggess?" asked Sir Bombardis. "I don't know, the giant was killed in a love triangle and Xaggess disappeared," answered the king as he walked out of the bedroom followed by Sir Bombardis to assemble the soldiers.

Through the blundering echoes of earthquakes and the sound of falling buildings the Dark Wolves waited patiently after hearing the loud thunder transpiring from high above. The moment had arrived for them to escape their prison and to prevail through the immortality of life. Rampant looked at his small band with swift assuredness that they would not be locked in this dark pit forever. "Don't worry my friends we will be set free and with great freedom we will cleanse the world!" Suddenly the prison was breached with falling rock and the Dark Wolves fluttered their wings. They screeched in great praise as they flew out of the pit and into the world of Ayana.

Furrengee sat down cross-legged in Humming Forest, next to the beautiful waterfall that filled a small, but ravishing stream with the reflection of the moon. The giant hand touched the ground. He let Aarilina move gently out of his immense fingers. Her smooth agile body was clean and white. She crawled along the ground like a wounded bird as her eyes slowly looked up at the towering mask that looked below. Her heart began thumping and thumping as the thought thickened of how to escape. Princess Aarilinus quickly panned her head down to the ground since it was too frightening to look upon the giant. Suddenly, the princess stared at the giant consumed with long, black, hair and black armor. The monarch feared for danger if such brown, innocent, eyes dared to look in the eyes of the mask would she be transformed. The myth from her bed time story suddenly came alive and was kneeled before her. Aarilina wondered if she would suddenly wake up from this dream or find herself visited by another bedtime character. Aarilina remembered the stories well, read to her by Jenna when she was only eight years old.

Minutes went by until her senses revealed it was not a dream and that the dream came true. Aarilina did not runaway like she planned and became brave while turning her exquisite eyes to get a better look at the leviathan that had gallantly rescued her. Who was this person that had come? The question haunted the princess' mind as her cheeks grew numb and lips trembled with high hopes. Maybe it was the mystery in the dream she had last night that began to fill Aarilina with excitement. Father told her that Animus was gone forever, which shattered the good heart that held Animus' face in such a beautiful mind. If Animus was gone who was this masked giant that seemed to read her psyche and know exactly that she was in the High Tower. The voices emanating from the mask were both men and women and could be heard in Aarilina's ears as a million voices. They weren't the voices of Animus and this fueled the princess' mystery even more. She could not understand what they meant or what they were saying and could not make them out in words. Only in thoughts did a thousand images of men and women appear to have all the answers to endless questions.

"Who are you?" she demanded. "Someone who would die to be in your arms!" a familiar voice replied.

Furrengee got up from his cross-legged position and slowly began shrinking until he was eye to eye with the princess. The armor began to disappear and the giant put a finger over his mouth as though meaning to hush while slowly renouncing the metal mask from his face. Beautiful flashes of light illuminated over the mask and went in all different directions as it was just over his face. He pulled the mask down just below his chin, unmasking his identity. His hair was the same length as it was before. He still had the dreamy, blue, eyes of a prince and the facial feature of a boy in love. "Animus!" embraced Princess Aarilinus surprised and emotional as she hugged him. "Aarilina!" cracked Animus. "I thought you were dead!" "Well I was close to being dead, but I was able to escape." "Animus how can you forgive me for all the rotten things I said to you?" "Even you have to admit that's pretty difficult for your father to break us apart. I'm not going to let something untrue bother me," replied Animus.

The two were together, now, forever through eternity. They hugged and kissed like never before with undamaged yearn for sempiternity. These lovers were made for each other and no nullity could break it. She looked in his eyes, her smile answered to a hundred wishes since the first day she laid eyes on him. He touched her back with his fingertips as they came closer to each other exquisitely. She touched his chest and neck with her finger nails, the way Animus longed for it. "What is this power you have found?" Aarilina whispered with fascination to her hero. Animus looked at the mask that was in his hands and had to remind himself that it was real. "It is the key to your heart, The anthem to a choir, the jewel to your father and the key to the locked doors of power. With this mask I will marry you and we will rule the kingdom together!" Aarilina grinned at Animus with her eyes, which enchanted whispers of secrets to his heart. Her hair was attractive as well as the soft white skin that rubbed up against his chest. She cracked a grin as her bangs crowded over such a fine-looking appearance. The two looked at each other for a long time and wondered where to begin. While there eyes met each other they sensed the others desire and knew their needs were met, now that they were together.

With the stare of the moon Animus could find no words comparable to Aarilina's elegance. The moon became just the moon and the perfect face became more than the water he drank on the farm. Animus touched the beautiful expression of open lips as the princess closed her eyes. It was smooth as it was soft, yet it remained hard and sculpted as great as the creator had planned to build. Aarilina leaned down from sitting on his stomach to touch his lips with hers. It was sweet as it was gracious and all she could do was beg for more. Freedom to do what they wished became reality in their world.

The mask, once worn by a great warrior, helped tie feelings of passion for each other. Aarilina laid her head upon Animus' chest and heard his heart beat, which sent her dreams of despair away into the darkness of the night. There were plans to watched the rise of the sun as the sky displayed the birth of a new day.

"Tell me you love me," whispered Aarilina with every syllable that plucked such lips. "I love you," the voice of the farm boy versed back in lullaby. "I love you too," with a kiss the light touched the peasant's chest. "Tell me about the mask, how does it work?" she asked. "Well," began Animus. "When I wear it I can feel a consciousness that I have never felt before. Millions of voices, memories, decisions made sometimes with or without my consent and sometimes before I realize it. The mask of Furrengee is made up of countless lovers who had loved many times before. That is what makes the mask so strong. The mask can bring back past lovers who have died. All that matters is how badly you loved them. The facade can't be used to attack offensively only defensively. It's like the spirits inside the mask would not let me destroy them. I could only put a curse on them and made the contraptions blow up. When the soldiers attacked me, the millions of love spirits put the curse on them with me which doubles the power," cracked Animus. "Incredible," Aarilina grinned.

Animus got up from lying on the leaves with Aarilina. The night was anticipating, transforming itself from dark blue to light blue. With the surface of the moon still in sight, Animus felt the aching in his soul. What if he was dreaming and would awaken back in the temple. Animus pinched himself and realized he was not dreaming. "I should protect you now, I'm vulnerable when I don't wear the mask." Aarilina got up and rested her head upon Animus' shoulder and imagined no day without him. They would not be separated again and father would try to kill Animus, but she would die for him. Aarilina would cascade through a rain of fire for him if it meant that they would remain one. "Animus lets runaway from here," Aarilina began with the trembling in her voice. "Runaway with me. I have nothing here and I want you, I need you!" she repeated.

Animus cracked his mouth and was about to pick up the mask from the tree stump when Aarilina stood in front of him. Her eyes glazed into his with the simple kiss to such firm lips. There was only the rich imagination of being together under the waterfall. Suddenly the princess' voice penetrated the night with the emotion of water splashing into a pond. "Tell me you love me!" "I love you with all my heart's desire," replied Animus. "Then lets runaway together!" exclaimed Aarilina. "We will after I face your father with the mask." "You are so touched. How do you know my father will keep his word?" "I believe he's going to want the mask enough to keep me alive," began Animus as he starred endlessly into her eyes like a diamond upon stars. "Besides you need to be crowned queen of Aria." "No I don't! Not with a father such as mine." "The people of Aria need you. You give them hope, dreams, happiness, joy, forgiveness, justice and the ability to choose what Aria wants." "Say that again, that was beautiful." "Imagine what power awaits you, my princess, after I face your father with the mask then you can execute the goodness shown before you."

Animus moved Princess Aarilinus aside as his eyes looked at the mask while the thought of King Ruke Owen took its shape in his mind. He thought about how hard he worked to possess the mask with so many hardships against him. His eyes turned to the metal mask forged by the warrior and the souls that possessed it. Animus kneeled down to pick up the mask and felt its smooth exterior. Suddenly he was stricken with fear as an arrow embedded itself into the hollow eye piece of the mask. The thought to grasp the mask soon withered in agony as sweat perspired from every pore, which sent shivers up his spine. The peasant's eyes shattered as his jaw began to shake to the tyrant staring upon him. In all desire to destroy Animus with one stroke of an iron fist the thought of the king emerged. Ruke would bring victory against the one who caused the destruction to the beautiful nation. The king would get revenge against the farmer for taking his daughter.

Animus raised his head slowly as such eyes lifted to the large number of knights slowly enclosed around him. The sun lifted from the distance against Animus' back while dawn embraced him into the new day. In eyes that begged for the encouragement of what was meant to be his. He felt the metal exterior of the king's sword as well as the significant loss of Aarilina. Slowly the sky unfolded to a dark blue with the sun peering from the horizon. The archers stood before the peasant with their crossbows aimed and ready to strike. Thoughts unraveled like a house of cards, which was comparable to an empty heart. Animus felt the thoughts warning him in the weight of his legs shaking in fear. Then as he sighed with the wind of Humming Forest that there may still be a way, he felt the mask within his reach. Humming Forest was the place of bonding with Aarilina that revered in a memory of eternity. Animus looked into the princess' eyes and saw how frightened she was. Only one answer emerged in Animus' mind, which was the moment where the mask would change the king's mind forever. Suddenly Animus heard the sound of a horse gruffing in the distance as the peasant looked deep into the forest and saw more men on horses hiding within the trees. Animus recognized one of the men that crept out as King Owen. His soldiers stepped out from hiding behind him and joined their king.

It was in this moment that Animus felt his triumph back fired The king would have him killed and steal the mask. Animus took a step towards the king as hate stared him down with the sound of a growl. The men on horses closed in at about twenty feet around the lovers and stretched their arrows back upon their wooden bows. "Not another step, peasant. I won't hesitate to have you killed!" began King Owen as he looked At Prince Tusk, Prince Domineer, Prince Lordoriouse, Prince Rubin and Prince Corsair. Animus knew without the mask he would be unable to become Furrengee. Everything that he has ever known to be good would be lost. Suddenly, Animus remembered something that his father told him. *If no one stood up against the king then no one would*! "You're quite a survivor farmer, I torched your home, killed your family, threw you to the Dark Wolves and you just keep turning up." "You are a liar!" answered Animus in anger for he knew the laws of the kingdom that no home on a claimed land would be destroyed. "Father how could you?" demanded Aarilina. "Daughter do we have to get back into this topic again of why?" "I told you I'm never going to marry any of the men you've chosen for me!" exclaimed the princess "Aarilina bring the mask and come along," King Owen demanded as he looked around to the trees and the sound of chirping birds.

Animus looked around in fear at the knights and saw anger in their eyes. His eyes met with Prince Tusk and felt hatred from him. He was the same man that delivered Aarilina's message. It suddenly made since that Prince Tusk knew where his family lived and left them to burn to death. Prince Tusk glared back at him with his mighty, brown, eyes as his night mare gruffed. "Father please--" begged Aarilina. "Come along and say good-bye!" interrupted the king.

The archers stretched their bows as Prince Tusk, Prince Domineer and Prince Rubin stretched their bows, loaded with an arrow in each string. They may as well shoot the peasant and Aarilina for the sin that was witnessed by King Owen. Aarilina turned to Animus as such eyes twinkled like the stars and watched Animus' eyes shine back. Something inside her knotted up like a string and the princess felt her heart split in two. She could feel it in the goose bumps along her neck, the fear of expecting the fiery will of another person's hate. Aarilina wasn't going to loose him again, she would take a hundred lashes to the death if it meant saving him. Aarilina imagined taking the mask back to Animus and unleash its power of greatness.

With the fine touch of lovely hands she grabbed the mask and felt its smooth metal texture of a warrior that wore it thousands of years ago. Animus wore this mask, would the same be bestowed upon him as a great, heroic, warrior of the land. With each step Aarilina made came the voice of her mother telling her the will of her heart. She felt the power as her eyes welled up with tears and that love would endure fear.

In Aarilina's mind she felt her mother walking near. The great queen's ghostly image, standing foot on end, held her hand that held the mask. With such assurance Aarilina feared nothing more than death itself and prepared each step faster to father. She sensed with the lightning strike in her back and the numbness in her jaw that Prince Tusk was going to fire his arrow anytime.

With great speed she turned around and branched each leg apart in a motion she never knew a princess could possess. In slow motion, she watched Animus open his arms as a crack from his grin opened up. Suddenly, it began to frown with sadness as Aarilina felt something strike her back. Something sharp and wicked ran its heat through her left shoulder blade. It thrusted itself out the middle of her chest as she continued to try and breathe. Blood dispersed from the wound like a river through a meadow. Princess Aarilinus had seconds before she would lay to rest while the words slipped through her lips. Aarilina closed her eyes with the feeling of pain as she took her final breath. "Runaway Animus! Hate strides behind there eyes like knives!" "Aarilina! Come back to me!" cried Animus as he cradled her in his arms. She was so fragile, weak and innocent. What service could a farm boy offer her. "No. Please no!" cried Animus.

With shaken legs and trembling arms he laid her down along the ground. He felt the volcanic anger erupt as he buried his face on her abdomen. The greatest thing in his life was lost, forever. Animus looked up at the king as his watered eyes and red face shared no comfort for any man present. The king already had his hands full screaming and yelling at Prince Tusk for shooting his arrow prematurely at Animus only to hit his daughter. "I am going to have you executed!" exclaimed King Ruke Owen. "You will do nothing of the sort for my father will declare war against Aria and I give you my word that my father will wipe you out!" "You fool I will have you castrated and fed to the Dark Wolves before your father even misses you!" "Would you like to solve our differences now!" declared Prince Tusk as he pulled out his sword. Sir Norcom and Sir Voles pulled out their swords as other soldiers turned their directions to the rogue prince. The king shook his head in disappointment and completely understood why his daughter didn't want to marry Prince Tusk.

"Lay your sword down sir." ordered Sir Norcom. "Are you deaf?" asked King Owen as he stared deep into the princes' dark, brown, eyes. "LAY DOWN YOUR SWORD!"

Prince Tusk threw down his weapon upon the ground and turned his eyes back to the sight of the king's angry eyes. Never before did Prince Tusk expect to have the king rise against him. "You will leave these grounds affective and immediately. I'm merciful this once for the threat you have made against my life, but you will be slayed upon sight if you are seen at my castle!" exclaimed King Owen. "This is war!" answered Prince Tusk as he rode off through the night on his black stallion. The king had made it quite clear that there would be no mistakes and his daughter would not be harmed. Prince Tusk had broken that rule and now would be banished from the beautiful nation.

King Owen turned to his faithful princes' and looked deep into their eyes. He promised each of them a challenge to retrieve the mask and marry his daughter. Now he would have to break that promise and risk going to war with them. "I regret to inform you that I must have you leave me in peace. I have lost my daughter and have no challenge!" "You've given me the opportunity to meet your future queen," replied Corsair. "Yes," answered the others. "She did have a lot of qualities that other women don't have," answered Lord Lordoriouse. "Princess Aarilina was a woman that perceived herself as not giving herself to anyone," began Lord Domineer. "I'll be leaving now," began Prince Rubin as he nudged his head to Sir Sebastian. "The loss of a man's daughter deserves to grieve on his own. It should not invite the intentions of others."

All five Princes were gone and King Owen had a new problem. A peasant was staring at him with anger and held the mask tightly in his hands. A drop of sweat began running down the side of the king's forehead. Animus laid her down on the grass as he heard the king mutter among the knights and archers. The beat of the horses' hoofs ran in the distant filled the peasants ears, but nothing could prepare him for the loss of what laid before him. Animus weeped and set his head upon the princess' stomach.

Anger for the right reason surfaced in his great, blue, eyes towards the ones that took Aarilina away. Animus raised his head up and stared at the king with eyes so vengeful that it made his heart ach. With such hatred what would it do for his soul? Animus suddenly heard his father's voice. A single beat with his heart as such word of wisdom entered the boy's ears. *The mask would not allow any offensive attack through its possession only in defense against great evil would it prevail.* The mask of Furrengee surely would have to let him take the lives of the loveless that took his ardor, beginning with the king. Who cares if the fiduciaries would vaporize his soul rather than take advantage of the positive power. Why not burn the rules and step on the king with a giant foot. His cheeks veered in a red rouge as his eyebrows slouched downwards. He could feel the numbness in the parts of his back as the tightness persisted in his clenched fist. "Animus, now wait a minute," began the king as he watched Animus touch and look at the mask. He pondered in thought about its power and wondered if the legend was true. Did Adam, his father, actually wear it? Animus looked into its eye piece and saw someone who looked like him with long, black, hair. Images of a young handmaiden who was his mother was also shown. It was his parents when they were young. "I meant no harm to my own daughter, I love her." "Just as you would love to see her life spent on someone you deemed worthy. Yea you just wanted to kill me and marry Aarilina to a better suited man!" screamed Animus. "Animus I apologize, but seeing you marry my daughter and run the kingdom does not settle in my stomach. Nobody would ask a farmer how to engage in war with another kingdom and no thanks to you I just declared war against Prince Tusk." "You arrogant, foolish, pig! How dare you display ignorance because of you Aarilina is dead, because of you I was banished for loving her, because of you I retrieved the mask of Furrengee to prove myself and because of you I will do what must be done," declared Animus as his eyes glared deep into the king's eyes. "I curse you old man. I curse you all, with the power to understand and accept me for who I am!" The peasant cried as he kneeled down and gripped Aarilina's right arm.

Animus continued to stare at the king with all but one thought on his mind of taking a life. He would will himself to return the princess to life as she was before the piercing of her heart. The king would be given these memories of the past childhood along with Adam's visit to the castle. Before the king would speak a word of condemning. A flood of these memories would rule his mind and haunt him for the rest of his life. "Today she was my soul mate and today the princess will be my wife!" exclaimed Animus.

All was quiet because the fate of Aria was in question. King Owen feared what power the mask would unleash. The toll unveiled upon the kingdom would be final. Animus placed the mask over his face and right away the magical armor and cape indulged once again. His hair grew long and dark while emulating the great warrior. He did not grow into a giant to crush the king and his men. Animus picked up Aarilina's limp body and pulled the arrow from her heart. He quickly placed his hand over the wound, which healed and lifted her body over his head. For a long time the mask began to flicker tons of white light, brighter than the sun, which touched everyone's eyes. Faces and voices spoke through the deaf ears of injustice.

The sweet innocent voice of the queen, Aarilina's mother, began walking towards Animus. The peasant watched the shadow walk towards him and knew very well who she was. She kneeled down as a soul to the limp, splitting image of the queen and began whispering her daughter's name. "Aarilina," spoke the queen slowly as her glowing face hovered over her daughter. "Aarilina open your eyes and return to your place as queen of Aria," replied the beautiful figure as she touched her daughter's neck. With a slight smile she bent down and whispered into the princess' ear. "Aarilina."

Suddenly Aarilina opened her great, brown, eyes to the sight of the rekindled queen kneeled down before her. It was amazing, Aarilina didn't want to breath because the sight of how beautiful her mother was. It was like the sound of harps playing in harmony to an unimaginable sunrise. The princess turned her head to see the power of the glowing mask. It blinked off and on with the color of white water dripping out of the eye holes. Some as Animus' own tears.

The mask's white light grew brighter and stronger to reach all of the archers, trackers, knights, guardians and hunters. They watched as they soon shed their tears of the wrong they had done. It was the emotions expressed by the mask of all the people who possessed the facade in the past. The king stared at the blur clusters of bright light that showered into his eyes. Memories clustered outwards into his mind as images of both his daughter's past and Animus' past combined. It revealed everything of why a princess would deem Animus as more than perfect.

Understanding Aarilina's heart's desire was Animus and realized as king he would have shattered his daughter like glass for forcing her heart upon another. He was wrong to think that a poor boy's heart was unworthy for a princess. Especially for a daughter fit to be queen. He witness the greatness of Aria as well as Aarilina's voice to motivate the people of Aria to win a war against the forces of evil. Was the prophecy of a Brokenheart destroying Aria a hoax? Maybe the prophets were mistaken?

The flashes of white light stopped and the queen that visited her daughter was gone. Animus looked at the princess as she slowly turned her eyes and head to the sight of sunlight. She was alive with a healed heart and grimaced a fragile smile to the knights as well as father. King Owen jumped off his horse quickly as excitement filled his body to hold her in his arms. Animus slowly brought Aarilina back to her feet again to renounce the mask from his face revealing the blue eyes and blonde hair that remained as true as his heart. Many of the knights and soldiers began running to the princess in great relief that she was alive. "I'm so sorry! Will you ever find it in your heart to forgive me!" cried King Owen as he held her in his arms. It was magic that she awoke from the dead and it was just amazing. No king would ever expect a son or daughter to come back to life after taking an arrow through the heart. "Of course I forgive you father," she answered with assurance and set her royal hand upon father's shoulder. "Father I saw my mother in my passing!" "I was told by her that she's waiting for you. What does that mean?" "It doesn't matter. What matters is that you're alive," answered King Owen. "I love you." The words spilled out like the sound of wolves howling in cries. "I'm in debt to you Animus for saving my daughter's life. It seems to me that you are the only match for my daughter and I welcome you to my kingdom." "I don't know what to say?" replied Animus in shock for he didn't believe that the legend was true. "Say you'll accept," cracked King Owen.

That morning preparations were made by the king for Animus to be knighted and crowned king. Thousands of people witnessed the peasant kneeled before King Owen. As the king slowly pulled out his royal sword Princess Aarilinus watched father brush the sword up against the young man's two shoulders.

It felt like a dream, who would have thought King Owen would be knighting a peasant. Animus' family was present at the knighting ceremony and waived their hands in high spirits. They were all dressed in satin and silk, the finest of noble clothing to witness such a gracious event. "Rise, Sir Animus Brokenheart," cracked King Owen as he watched the knight rise up with the shiny, silver, armor. The wind brushed up against the long, blonde, hair in different directions as Animus faced the people he was sworn in to defend. The crowds cheered while clapping their hands and with the huge wave of love for him the knight bowed with a smile on his face.

Princess Aarilinus stepped out in the sun with Sir Animus Brokenheart. She was dressed in the red, satin, color dress with a gold belt and was wearing a pearl necklace. The golden crown sparkled against the glimmer of the sun. It was not shining as much as the smile on her face. "I've got to go," replied Aarilina "Go where?" asked Animus. "My handmaidens have dresses for me to look at and try on," she cracked and bestowed a kiss upon the knight's lips.

Animus watched her run away inside the corridor of the castle with about ten handmaidens. The knight was ecstatic and couldn't wait to see her again. He turned his head to the cheering crowds and pulled out his sword to raise it in the air. The crowd went wild and it sent excitement through his bones.

After hours passed and preparations were being made to wait. Animus turned around to see his father with a grin on his face. "Father!" said Animus. "I'm happy that your alive son and want you to know that I'm very proud of you!" "Thank you, I never knew something like this would happen to me." "It did! Does it make you happy, Sir Animus?" "Well I'm soon to be crowned king this late afternoon, but yes I'm very happy with what has transpired today." "What about you?" began Animus. "What do you and mom got planned?" "Well we're going to go away on a special adventure while your brothers and sisters are taken care of by Aarilina's father. I do have one question what was it like walking around the citadel?" asked Adam as he crossed his arms. "It was like a special adventure," smirked Animus as he shook Adam's hand and looked forward to the hour.

The church packed with people of all ages, but soon it came near for Aarilina to walk down the aisle. She was dressed in white with slivers of gold, silver and blue through out the dress. The white veil covered her perfect face and King Owen stepped beside his daughter as they marched. He was dressed in his fancy clothes with golden necklaces. His long red cape was dragged behind him as his crown fit perfectly over his head. "You look like your mother," replied King Owen as he held her hand tightly. "Thank you, father." Aarilina answered as she kissed him on the cheek. She knew father was nervous, but with a grin she focused such eyes to Animus. Animus was dressed like a prince with silky clothes and his hair combed nicely. The princess felt a strange knot in her stomach and suddenly a tear fell upon her cheeks. Aarilina felt herself fit in a dream that would never let her wake up. The presence of her mother walking side by side made the day more admirable. They were face to face and felt each other's hearts beating together. Minutes seemed to swing by fast as Animus and Aarilina listened to their vows. Animus unraveled the veil to see the princess' porcelain face and witnessed such wonderful eyes looking at him. He dried her cheeks with his finger after hearing, "You may kiss the bride." The prince cracked and leaned to the princess. He took Aarilina in his arms and kissed her, realizing that this day was never leaving his memories.

The two began running down the aisle as rice was thrown at them. The doors opened and they made their way to the carriage chased by loved ones. The carriage door closed and they rode off to the castle and stopped to the stable. "Animus what are we doing?" asked Aarilina. "You wanted to run away together. This is our chance!" cracked Animus as he led the way to two white stallions. "Ohh Animus they're beautiful, but where did you get them?" "They were brought here as a present from Prince Corsair who found out you were alive, but couldn't attend." "Where shall we go?" "There are some mountains overlooking the bluffs just east of here. I thought by that time we could watch the sun set." The two jumped on their white stallions and trotted off from the stall led by Animus. The castle gates opened up and Aarilina imagined herself free as a bird, free from the cage that held her captive. Animus cracked as the wind brushed up against such cheeks, knowing forever the mask had changed their life.

It was dusk and Ruke Owen sat on his bed, under the covers, writing the diary. There was a knock at the door and the king raised his eyes as he set the feathered pen back in the ink. Ruke shut the book and slid it under his pillow and sat up before preparing for whoever would enter the room. The sound of the knock persisted until the king finally cleared the roughness in his voice.

"Come in."

The door opened and Adam appeared before the king. King Owen's eyes widen in surprise for he didn't expect the rogue warrior to talk to him. Adam looked at the king with kind eyes, with honorable eyes. They were filled with sorrow and regret for the past as well as what was revealed from King Owen.

"My son is very happy. I haven't seen him happy like this for a long time," smiled Adam. "What made you decide to allow Princess Aarilina to marry Animus?" "I was wrong about your son," began King Owen. "Animus saved my daughter's life. I hope someday you can forgive me for what wrong I have unleashed upon you in your past." "I forgive you," answered Adam after a couple minutes of silence. "Thank you," grimaced King Owen as he watched Adam turn around to leave. "Nobody is perfect and I'm happy that the cold bitterness is gone between us," replied Adam as he turned around to watched King Owen crack a grin before closing the door.

Ruke Owen pulled the diary back out again and began writing his thoughts of the day that would never end. Suddenly he heard something peculiar from his left and slowly turned to see the mask was near. The voice was Queen Aarilinus, long deceased had she been and now she was speaking to him. *Come to me my lord.* The words seemed to bury themselves inside of him like a lamp. He tried to ignore the voice that entered his mind and cut off any sense of hope that the mask actually worked. King Owen turned his head to the mask just as he heard the feminine voice again and saw the beautiful face appear in his wonderful mind. *Don't be afraid of me and don't be afraid of the light.* King Owen turned his head forward to see it was her. She stood before him looking as beautiful as the day that ended for him. Her brown eyes looked upon him with the grimace upon such a gorgeous face. Queen Aarilnus bowed her head to the king. "Ruke come with me," she exclaimed while holding her arms and hands out.

King Owen rose out of bed to step towards her and hoped she was not a dream. She was smiling at him and waiting to be held in his. Ruke touched her hand with his and realized that Aarilina, his wife, was real. The sound of a heart beat was the most beautiful thing that entered his ears as he realized his head was near her chest. "My lord Ruke there's a place that we can go to live in peace!" she replied while opening her mouth. *Come. Come into the light. Come into the light my lord Ruke.* Her thoughts embraced his.

The King's Retribution

The next morning was a day of mourning for King Owen. Countless numbers of subjects attended the funeral. It was a dark day for the kingdom as they lowered the casket into the ground. The lovers were dressed in black clothes and the knights carried out the new queen's orders. Animus held Aarilina during this time of tears and felt how unprepared she was for father's departure. "I didn't get a chance to say good-bye," cried Aarilina. "It's all right," assured Animus as he looked through her black veil and knew that he would be there to comfort her.

The sun poked out from the bluffs in the distance, which showed a beautiful sunrise. Images of father tossing her up in the air as a child appeared in Aarilina's mind. She could still hear her own laughter from the time of a young girl. The days of chasing after her in play, to tickle her. Despite the image he held that presented itself as evil, King Owen loved her very much. He aloud Aarilina to play with the children when she was younger and explore the castle. "Your father would have wanted you smiling for your future" replied Animus. "I didn't expect him to leave so soon," she sobbed. "He didn't leave you. He's watching us just as your mother has been watching you all your life. You are going to be a powerful queen that will inspire the people of Aria to do wonderful things," answered Animus as he wiped the tears from Aarilina's eyes. "Your right," she wiped her eyes and looked into Animus' grin. "Look at what is created for us!" exclaimed Animus as they both looked at a rainbow in the sky over the most beautiful sunset ever seen. "He's here with us. I can feel it," declared Aarilina as the biggest grin revealed itself in a laughter over the pain.

Suddenly Aarilina saw the beauty that the day brought for that instant. She let a smile emerge from her face and let out a laugh. Aarilina could feel the old king and queen leave them now. She closed her eyes and imagined them waving good by as they ascended into the air. Queen Aarilinus and King Animus stepped into the reality that was more than a dream. It had only begun.

The End

I would like to thank god for being by my side while writing this manuscript. I would like to thank my mom and dad, Karen and Lynde, for believing in me. I would also like to thank my sisters Ariane, Stephanie and Kayla. Without you I wouldn't be where I am now, god bless you. I would also like to thank Corrine (Cheetah), Robert Harris, Kisus Ann Metoxen, Lisa Hildebrandt, Ms. Murphy, Lisa Steiner, Mr. Frautschi, Naomi Pidd, Ms. Rose Erickson, Nancy Klass, Mary Olson, Alice Stout, Jeff Hanson, Cheryl Boden, Gabe Whall, Chris Lee, Linda Mancheski, Ms. Bongers, Jeff Pierson, Ms. Morse, Shannon Barkley, Deb Zeilsdorf, Dave Hanson, Freddy Henzler, Karin Dillner, Stephanie Grimm, Kathy Kleinhans, Kathy (or cat), Jeremy Gilbert, Dave Herr, Darren Corbin, Mrs. Irlebeck, Dave Hunt, Mike Van Ness, Keith Moyer, Lori Johnson, Darlyn Thomas, Chad Hill, Robert Norton, Adrian Bravo, Lars Ulrich, Jason Newstead. I would like to thank Professor Harold Scheub for taking the time to talk to me about publishing and giving me his book. Special thanks for musical inspiration by Jane Siberry and Sarah Brightman for the writing of the manuscript. I would like to thank who ever I didn't mention (you know who you are).

Special thanks for being in my workshop:
Mary and Marty Fagnan
Linda Narveson
Dan Aluni of Mystic Suns

Erica Fuss (As Usual)
Cathy Paguin

Additional editing by Margaret Hunt. Love letter, illustration and poem created by Ryan Johnson.

Synopsis

In the world of Ayana was a kingdom called Aria. King Owen ruled Aria, alone, for seventeen years since his queen passed away. He cared for Princess Aarilinus who was most precious and beautiful woman in the land. King Owen was a man with a terrible past of anger, regret as well as greed.

The king of Aria has a problem. Aarilina is in love with Animus who is not only a peasant, but is son of the man who is responsible for the death of the queen, Aarilina's mother. There is great tension and frustration between King Owen and his daughter.

Animus is challenged to retrieve a mask with many other suitors to marry the princess. The mask, once worn by a great warrior makes the possessor invincible to any army. The mask is heavily guarded by creatures of the darkness within the citadel. The king hopes to trick Animus into self dought, but soon finds that the temple will do the work of destroying him. King Owen knows that the mask has a history of its own and discovers the truth that love is the strongest feeling in the world.

Authors Biography

Ryan Keith Johnson was born in Stillwater, Minnesota and grew up in Somerset, Wisconsin. Ryan has been writing since he was 13 years old and hasn't stopped creating interesting plots. Water color painting, ink illustration as well as using pastel has been an inspiration to capture his imagination.

Ryan began with the publishing of his poem in 1996 in the Anthology of Poetry for Young Americans. He graduated from Brown College in 2000, with the emphasis in graphic design. His inspiration for writing comes from listening to Celtic music as well as Nichole Nordemen, Michael W. Smith, Jane Siberry, Sarah Brightman and other Christian music.

When he's not writing he enjoys nature hikes, swimming on the beach, watching a good movie, exercising and relaxing. Creating a personal relationship with Jesus is very extraordinary and can only be accomplished by inviting Him into your life. Helping people is a task that is also enjoyable. Ryan plans to publish more Christian books as well as sell his water color paintings, and complete his collaboration of a graphic board game.

www.ingramcontent.com/pod-product-compliance
Lightning Source LLC
LaVergne TN
LVHW041713060526
838201LV00043B/718